# Queenie in Seven Moves

# Queenie in Seven Moves

### Zanni Louise

CANDLEWICK PRESS

First US edition 2025
First published by Walker Books Australia 2023

Library of Congress Control Number: 2024944030
ISBN 978-1-5362-3583-8

25 26 27 28 29 30 SHD 10 9 8 7 6 5 4 3 2 1

Printed in Chelsea, MI, USA

This book was typeset in Chaparral Pro.

Candlewick Press
99 Dover Street
Somerville, Massachusetts 02144

www.candlewick.com

EU Authorized Representative: HackettFlynn Ltd.,
36 Cloch Choirneal, Balrothery, Co. Dublin, K32 C942, Ireland.
EU@walkerpublishinggroup.com

*To the Armytages, the McAllisters,*
*and the Altices*

# HØME

## one

**MY CHEST IS TIGHT. I CLUTCH MR. GREY'S GUITAR** like it's going to fly away.

This is it. My final chance to get on the Brown & Jolly Stage and knock 'em dead.

*I can do this. I can really do this.*

I peek out from the wings. My entire school faces me. I see Mrs. Doherty, the principal, sitting in the front row, her expression terse. Dread feels like Antarctica on a winter's day.

*I can do this. I have to do this.*

This is the furthest I have ever made it. Usually, I chicken out before signing up for the concert. But this year, Mr. Grey gave me the guilt treatment in epic proportions.

"Queenie, I have been teaching you now for nearly seven years. You're the best guitarist I've ever taught. Yet you're the only kid I've ever taught who refuses to perform. Do you want to make my entire teaching experience pointless? This is it, kiddo. After this, there is no end-of-year school concert. Just the upper school. And you know what that's like."

I don't know what it's like. But I do know what it's like to carry Mr. Grey's guilt. It's a weighty object, and he's been putting it on my shoulders every year since I made him cry by fingerpicking "Moonlight Sonata."

So I did it. I told Mr. Grey I'd play a song at the end-of-year concert. Mr. Grey had already printed the posters. So he had to go out and do a reprint especially for me.

Quadruple guilt.

Max Rawling is currently belting out the final bit of "Bohemian Rhapsody" on melodeon. It's awful. But the kid's so confident. You've got to give him that.

"Good luck, Queenie," says Sparrow Hawkins, poking me in the ribs.

"Thanks," I mutter.

Thank goodness Sparrow is on after me.

If you looked at Sparrow, you wouldn't straightaway think she had the potential to be an archrival. She's so

4

friendly-looking, with her oversize mouth and shiny dark skin. Anyone who wears that many colorful beads in her hair should not be an archrival.

But ever since Sparrow and I stopped being best friends in kindergarten, when she told me she could sing better than me, I've done my best to keep out of her spotlight.

Sparrow the Fabulous. The Voice of Destiny.

Sparrow the Spotlight Stealer.

Sparrow will sing after me, and she'll be better than me. But for a moment, I'll own the spotlight, and I'll sing my favorite song, and Mr. Grey's guilt will slip off my shoulders, and I can proceed to the upper school weightless and victorious. I, Queenie Jean Anderson, performed at Curlew Point's end-of-year concert.

Mrs. Fig, head of the PTA and yearbook committee, is emceeing the annual concert. When Max finally departs the stage, Mrs. Fig strides on in cowboy boots.

"Thank you, Max. Marvelous. Simply marvelous. Aren't all our kids talented?" There's a polite clap and murmur from the students and supportive parents.

Mum's not out there today. Not because she's not supportive. But because she's at Diamonds, the senior care village where she works. She probably could have gotten out of her shift if she knew about the concert. But I decided to save her the hassle. Having Mum in the audience might have been more than my nerves could handle.

"And now for our next performance," Mrs. Fig reads from the little square of paper in her hand. She has to squint. My tummy rolls over. This is it. No escaping things now. "Sparrow Hawkins."

What? My throat tightens. I should call out. I should let Mrs. Fig know that she's wrong. It's supposed to be me, *then* Sparrow.

But Mrs. Fig is marching offstage and Sparrow is skipping on, her brand-new black guitar strapped to her back.

She positions herself center stage, feet hip-width apart. She flicks her braids from her face with an almighty whip.

"Go, Sparrow!" someone calls out.

Sparrow's everyone's favorite sixth grader. She's been shining on this stage since kindergarten.

Following Sparrow Hawkins is like being the over-cooked peas served *after* ice cream.

Disgusting and inferior. I'm not even a palate cleanser.

Sparrow strikes a few chords. People cheer.

The notes sink into me. I want to disappear. Evaporate.

She's singing "Ocean Eyes." She's singing my song. My favorite song. The song I am about to play straight after her in a less impressive way.

The first verse wraps around me, holding me hostage. By the chorus, I'm out of there. I slip out the side door and carry Mr. Grey's guitar back to the music room. Leaving is so ridiculously easy.

I spend the rest of the end-of-year concert by myself in the library, reading *Asterix and Obelix*, trying to distract myself from the hopeless case of pathetic I know I am right now.

## two

BETSY, OUR NEIGHBOR-SLASH-babysitter-slash-landlady, is sitting on her deck when I get home. Her wild hair is like a red mushroom. She's taken to dyeing her hair with henna, which is kind of cool and kind of weird, given how ordinary her clothes are.

"Rough day, Queenie?" she says, blowing on her green tea.

I shrug. "Nah," I say. Even though it was.

Betsy used to change my diaper. She's fed me cereal most of my life. She's packed my lunch boxes. She knows when I'm lying.

"How 'bout you give Garfield a kiss, hey?" she says. "He always makes the world a better place."

I scowl at Garfield, the ugly garden gnome at the bottom of her step. He grins back at me smugly.

"No, thanks," I say, and trudge past Betsy's to our place. And there she is. Peachy.

My beloved peach-walled beauty. Home. Solace. Love of my life.

She welcomes me like the peach mama she is, all art deco and flaky paint. I love her with my whole heart. If I could hug a house, I would hug Peachy.

Mum's back from work. She's at the kitchen table. Two takeaway hot chocolates are on the table—one with a marshmallow on the lid.

"Queenie Pants!" says Mum. She doesn't get up but hugs me with her eyes. "Take a seat for a sec. I have to chat with you about something."

"Maybe later," I say.

I eyeball my hot chocolate. The one with the marshmallow. If I accept the gift, I am entering into a transaction where I sit down with Mum and discuss my day. But all I want is to be alone in my room.

The walls shake when I slam my door.

I chuck my schoolbag on the floor and collapse on my bed. Out of the corner of my eye, I catch Dad's guitar in its stand. I squeeze my eyes shut to make it go away.

*Not now, Dad's guitar. Not now.*

I plug Billie Eilish into my ears and let her sound wash over me. Not "Ocean Eyes," of course. I won't be able to listen to my favorite song for months, probably years, because of Sparrow Hawkins.

The jacaranda is in bloom. It's late this year—usually it blooms in October. Its mauve flowers wave at my window, like little purple paws. Light filters through. If I squint, I could be snorkeling through coral reefs.

My breath slows.

Mum must have been watching the clock, because she gives me a good three songs before she eases open my door and lowers herself onto my bed. She hands me a hot chocolate—the one with the marshmallow. I nod *thanks*, swallow the marshmallow whole, and take a sip from the plastic lid. The chocolate is stone cold but deliciously sweet.

It almost definitely makes my day a bit better.

Mum watches me, waiting. The lines around her eyes crinkle. It's like she has something to say but she's thinking of the best words to use.

Uh-oh. Mum has a boyfriend.

No. Please no. Not today.

Not any day.

Mum's best friend, Sarah, who lives in London, has been trying to get Mum into online dating for the last few years. Thankfully, Mum says she's not ready.

Anyway, Mum doesn't need a boyfriend. She has me. Isn't that enough?

Mum's still not saying anything.

I could tell her about the concert, or the lack thereof. But she'll be mad at me for not inviting her.

"How was work?" I ask finally.

"Well, you know." She gazes out at the jacaranda. "Pretty, isn't it?"

"Mum?" I say. She's deferring. Dread uncoils in my stomach.

In another world, Mum should date. She's beautiful, for sure. And still young, for a mum. Also seven years is a very reasonable amount of grieving time.

But there's no other world. This is it.

"Betsy's sold the place," says Mum.

"What?" I yank out my earbuds. I knock over the takeaway cup. Liquid chocolate pools on the bedside table.

"Betsy's sold Peachy. We have to move."

Dread stretches—a cold wintry beast, reaching into every internal organ.

"She can't," I croak.

"She can. And she has."

Through the quiet, I hear Billie whispering away in my earbuds.

11

"Why can't we stay? Betsy doesn't have to stay. We can keep renting."

Mum shakes her head. "The new owners are moving in next week. Places are flying off the market, according to Betsy. Everyone wants to move out of the city because of the pandemic. Betsy got an offer she couldn't refuse."

I think of the couple that Betsy and some guy walked around the property with a few weeks ago. Mum had this urgent need to take me shopping, which at the time I thought was weird. But now I realize it was a way of extracting me from my beloved home.

I feel cheated.

"Next week! That's too fast! Shouldn't these things take months?"

Mum's gazing out the window again, avoiding eye contact.

I flip back through the last few weeks, looking for more clues.

Mum staying late at work. Mum spending more time on her phone. Mum leaving me with Betsy so she could get to a late-afternoon or weekend meeting.

I'd been trying to ignore the slim possibility that Mum could be dating.

She wasn't dating.

"You've known for a while," I say.

She nods and turns to me. Her dark eyes swim. "I've been looking for a place, Queenie. I didn't want to tell you until I found something perfect. Something you'd love, so you could get excited about the change. But I haven't been lucky. Now Betsy's pushed the moving date forward a week. I've run out of time."

"You should have told me," I say. "I could have helped you look!"

Mum purses her lips. "I know how you can be," she says softly.

Her words rock around for a bit. I won't lie. They hurt.

I prove Mum right by scowling and plugging Billie back in my ears. I turn toward the wall. Mum sits for a while. Eventually, I feel her sigh and leave the room.

"You better start thinking about packing," I hear her say somewhere in the distance.

*o o o*

My blip lasts all the way until dinnertime. It's amazing how much Billie you can listen to without ever getting sick of her.

My rumbling tummy gets the better of me. So does the smell of spaghetti Bolognese. Mum makes the best spag bol.

I pull my chair up to the table and eat wordlessly. Mum puts her hand on mine. I feel her eyes boring into me.

"Look. Don't say anything. Just listen. I need to tell you this. I just spoke to Sue. She's confirmed that we can move into Diamonds for a couple of weeks until we find our feet. There's a new resident moving in soon, but until then, we can use her apartment. How good is that?" Mum finishes with a grin.

I look up sharply.

"Diamonds? Really? Don't you have to be over eighty to live at Diamonds?"

"Well, over sixty, technically. But thirty-two is the new sixty!"

"What about me? I'm twelve."

"Oh, you're going to feel right at home," says Mum, her eyes dancing. "Grumpiness is all the rage in Diamond Sands Seniors Village."

A smile twinges at the corner of my mouth. I can't help it. "As long as *no one* ever finds out," I say. "And you've got to promise no one will die while we are there."

Mum cocks an eyebrow. "I'll do my best to keep everyone alive. Especially for you, Queenie Jean."

# three

**MUM ONLY LETS ME TAKE** one tiny roller bag and Dad's guitar to Diamonds. The rest is packed in a truck in cardboard boxes to be shipped to a storage unit. I watch after the truck as it teeters down Whittlesea Avenue.

"Goodbye, life," I say, waving.

Mum hangs her arm over my shoulder. "It'll be good for us. Being nomads. Didn't you ever want to roam about living in a camper van?"

"No," I say. "Never."

The only place I want to live is home. Peachy Home. Nowhere else.

"No, neither did I," says Mum. "Can't think of anything worse."

Betsy hobbles over. She comes up to my shoulder. She puts her arm around Mum's waist. I'm so mad at her, I could vomit on her scuffed loafers. Instead I stand stiffly.

"End of an era," says Betsy. Her stuff is getting picked up tomorrow morning. She's moving in with her daughter, who lives somewhere down south.

Mum kisses Betsy's mushroom hair. "I'll miss us," she says. "You've been good to us, Betsy."

Even though I don't like Betsy right now, it's true. She has been good to us. Without Betsy, Mum couldn't have started work at six a.m. every day. Without Betsy, Mum would have had to quit work altogether to look after me during the COVID lockdown.

Without Betsy, we wouldn't have Peachy.

And we wouldn't have lost Peachy.

I glare at the ugly gnome, who has yet to find a box, and know exactly what I need to do.

# the first move
# DIAMONDS

# four

**IT'S THE FIRST SATURDAY IN DECEMBER.** Our first official day without a home. We pull into the Diamonds parking lot. A resident hobbles up to us and slams his fist against my window. I jump. Mum winds down the window and leans across me.

"Hello, Duncan. How was your walk?" she says.

Duncan grins. Three teeth are missing. His sour breath fills our car. I try not to gag.

"S'good," says Duncan. "Heard you are moving in, Clare! That's lucky for us!"

"Lucky for Queenie and me, you mean!" says Mum. "Sue's my guardian angel." Duncan reaches across me, making a fist. Mum fist-bumps him, which makes Duncan giggle.

"Not lucky for us," I grumble.

Mum widens her eyes in mock surprise.

"Oh, she speaks! How charming. Here I was thinking we left your voice behind on Whittlesea Avenue."

"My voice. My heart. My everything." I glare across the dashboard.

"It's a good thing you aren't too dramatic," says Mum. "Otherwise I'd have to start calling you Drama Queenie."

My response is a gurgle from deep inside. Mum's still smiling at me, which is the worst.

Diamonds is a village of small units, each with their own porch and minuscule garden. It's toy town, blown up, each unit identical—neat and tidy. Each with a wheelchair ramp and lots of handrails for safety. There's one main building, for reception, staff offices, and a communal dining room for residents who like to eat together.

YOUR FOREVER HOME, it says under the Diamonds entrance sign.

OMG, I hope not.

Mum parks in front of the main building. I trudge after her, pulling my little wheelie bag with the busted zipper. Mum greets everyone we pass along the way. Caregivers, residents, family members. A tall woman called Meg, with shoes that look two sizes too big, hugs Mum.

"Welcome home, darling. I told you you'd never leave," she says. I grimace. "Oh, you must be the famous Queen!"

"Queenie," I say.

"I know. I'm just joking with you, Queenie. I know everything about you! Your mum can't stop singing your praises. You're a wonderful guitar player, your mum says!"

I death-stare Mum. She has no right to tell people my personal information!

A woman thumps toward us. She has a thin layer of beard, which is surprising to see on a woman. She wears the Diamonds navy-blue uniform. Her badge reads SUE TOWNSEND. Sue, the director at Diamond Sands, doesn't look much like a guardian angel, I think. Then I realize I am being mean.

"Greetings," says Sue, giving a salute.

"Sue!" says Mum. "Thanks again for letting us stay until Mrs. Lim arrives."

"Wouldn't let you end up on the street," says Sue. "Or let you pay a million dollars for an Airbnb. Not in this climate. I told you that Dave can't find a place, either, didn't I? He's moved in with me for the time being. God help me."

21

"Dave is Sue's son," Mum explains to me.

"You guys are in unit seventeen. The cleaner's been through. Treat it as your own."

Unit 17 is directly behind the main building. Neat, tidy, wheelchair ramp, handrails. A single topiary tree standing guard out front. Lawn so perfect it could be fake.

Mum jostles the key in the lock. Eventually, the door swings open.

"Well, this is us!" says Mum, way too cheerily.

The first thing I notice about the unit is that it smells strongly of Windex.

"What happened to the last resident?" I ask, giving the place a once-over.

Mum doesn't reply. She's pretending she didn't hear me. I can tell.

"Mum? The last resident? Did they move out?"

"Well . . . " Mum says slowly. She puts her bag on the bed and starts unfolding.

"They died, didn't they?" I say.

Mum puts a pile of her undies in the drawer beside the only bed.

"Yes, Queenie, John Johnson passed away in his sleep last weekend."

"Last weekend!" The unit suddenly takes on a whole new feeling. It's haunted! I can feel John Johnson's ghost practically stroking my shoulder. I shudder.

Mum tuts. "Don't be silly, Queenie. John Johnson died peacefully. And look, it happens. People pass away from time to time. It's an unfortunate part of the job."

All I can think is *two weeks*. Mrs. Lim moves into unit 17 in two weeks. Which means Mum and I have two whole weeks to find our new home.

I jiggle the broken zip and start unpacking my things into John Johnson's laminate wardrobe. Mum doesn't say anything when I perch Garfield the gnome on my bedside table. But I can see she's holding in a smile.

I'm not your regular thief. But somehow, this doesn't feel like thieving. It feels like justice. That's what you get, Betsy, for kicking a family out of their forever home.

## five

**I MAKE A LIST OF THINGS WE ARE LOOKING FOR** in our new forever home on the back of a discount store receipt:

1. *Must have a garden. Gardening is Mum's outlet.*
2. *Must be an old Queenslander type of house.*
3. *Must have wooden floors.*
4. *Must have a fireplace.*
5. *Must have a gas stove for Mum's spag bol.*
6. *Ideally has good acoustics and a spare room I can use as a music room.*

I show Mum the list on our way to dinner. She can't be bothered cooking tonight, so we'll be eating in the communal dining room with other residents.

She laughs, as if I am joking around.

"So where do we start looking?" I say. "Is there a place you go to find rentals? A real estate agency or something?"

"I've been looking on the real estate app every day, Queenie," says Mum. "There's not a lot out there."

"Can I look?" I reach for her phone, which is in her hand. Mum opens the app for me. She types "Curlew Point" in the search bar and chooses "Rental."

Three places come up. One is a brick-and-tile apartment. Totally wrong. Totally tiny.

One is an old Queenslander out in the hinterland. It has a pool and an archway. Totally amazing, but clearly way out of our league.

One is a house like Betsy's—small and dark, with linoleum floors. Would rather not.

I hand Mum back her phone.

The dining room also smells Windex-y. The scent is infused with sour cabbage. Old people sit gathered around round plastic tables, some hunched. Some poking at their food with cutlery.

We take the only two empty seats at a table in the middle of the room. Fake flowers float in a bowl of water in the center of the table.

Mum introduces me to Audrey, whose thin purplish hair is tied in a tight knot on the top of her head. Her wheelchair is pressed firmly into the table, so it looks like the table swallowed her.

"How old are you, Queenie?" asks Audrey after giving me a thorough inspection.

"Twelve," I say. I inspect the so-called potato mash that Meg slides in front of me. It looks and feels more like Styrofoam. "How about you?"

Audrey laughs. "Ninety-three."

"Wow! Ninety-three!" I stare at her. "That's impossible! I was going to say sixty or something."

"Gran's sixty!" says Mum from the other side of Audrey. "And she's dating a ski instructor in Toronto."

It's true. Gran moved to Toronto for love three years ago. Still no one can believe it.

"I could date a ski instructor if I wanted to," says Audrey.

Mum pats her hand. "I know you could, Audrey. But you'd have to fight off the Swedish massage therapist first."

"I'd prefer Arnie, actually," says Audrey.

"Who's Arnie?" I ask.

Audrey looks shocked. "You don't know Arnie? Literally the best-built Austrian man ever made. Ex-governor of California. The Terminator!"

"You mean Arnold Schwarzenegger?" I say. "That's hilarious."

26

Audrey shoots me a laughing look.

"Audrey could date me if she wanted to," says a man across the round table, who I realize now has been ogling us for the entire meal.

"Oh, Wayne, how many times do I have to remind you? You're married!" says Audrey. Wayne sighs and prods his mashed potato with a fork. "What would Marielle say if I stole her man?"

I cover my smile. I had no idea Diamonds was such a soap opera. All crushing and dating and stealing boyfriends.

"Marielle doesn't have to know! She has her own life back in Marrick Lake!" Wayne sure is serious about Audrey.

Audrey leans toward me so she can whisper. "Have you met Walter yet?" she asks.

"Who's Walter?" I whisper back. I feel like I'm about to get a real gem of Diamonds gossip.

Audrey taps the side of her nose.

"Let's just say, Walter is a BIG fan of underwear. Massive." Audrey smiles.

Underwear?

"Audrey, hush. You shouldn't gossip about the other residents like that," says Mum. "How would you feel if someone was gossiping about you?"

"I should hope they're gossiping about me!" says Audrey, flicking a wily strand of purple hair behind her ear.

After our Styrofoam dinner is cleared away, a guy walks into the dining room wearing only a pair of tighty-whities. He plonks into a chair by the unlit fireplace and reads his magazine. I figure the underwear man must be Walter. Audrey's suddenly gone really quiet and is looking out the window. I am trying to catch her attention by waggling my eyebrows to confirm I am right.

Mum kicks me under the table. Audrey doesn't see me anyway. She's somehow far more interested in the view out the window.

# six

**I AM SITTING ALONE AT RECESS,** with my back against the wall, when Sparrow Hawkins and her newest best friend, Lili Evans, approach. For a moment, I think they are going to sit with me. But then they sit a few benches away.

It's hard to believe now, but Sparrow used to be my best friend when we were little. We did everything together. Sleepovers. Birthdays. Holidays.

Sparrow had the best stuff at her house, like a trampoline and all the cool toys. And her mum was so nice to us, giving us heaps of food my mum would never let me eat at home.

We did these dumb shows for our parents. Shows we'd make up and dress up for. I remember one where

I was a news reader and Sparrow was the weather lady. Once, we rewrote "The Three Little Pigs." I was all the pigs and Sparrow was the wolf. The parents thought it was hilarious.

Then Sparrow started getting competitive.

It started when Mum took me to guitar lessons. Then Sparrow wanted a guitar.

Mum took me to singing lessons. Then Sparrow had to get singing lessons.

I didn't care that much. But I cared when Sparrow sang in my face and told me I should whisper because I couldn't sing very well.

It wasn't very nice.

We have music after recess. Mr. Grey is on stress leave apparently, so we have a substitute teacher—Miss Donaghy. I like Miss Donaghy straightaway. She's way younger than the other teachers. And she has a tattoo of a dragon curling up her arm. She's even got a nose ring and wears Doc Martens. She tells us to call her Daisy.

Not your usual Curlew Point schoolteacher.

"We're going to do some songwriting today," says Daisy. The class groans.

Only Sparrow Hawkins calls out, "Yes!" and pumps the air. "Love songwriting, Miss!"

Of course Sparrow loves songwriting.

The image of Sparrow onstage at the end-of-year concert pops into my head uninvited. Sparrow singing *my* song. The song I was meant to sing. Her eyes closed. Confidence oozing out of every beautiful pore.

"That's great, Sparrow!" says Daisy. "Love your name, by the way. Great name for a musician!"

Sparrow beams.

I scowl.

I notice Dory, the boy who just transferred from the Catholic school, slip out the door. He must be going to some chess tournament or something. Apparently, the boy is a chess wizard.

I've been playing guitar since I could toddle. But I've never played my own music—only other people's.

We have to get into pairs, which is one of my least favorite things to do in a classroom. As usual, Sally and I are the only people left without partners. The Unchosen Ones, I call us in my head.

"Will you be my partner, Queenie?" asks Sally. Her voice is rice-paper thin.

I shrug. "Yeah, I'll be your partner, Sally."

"We're just going to throw random words down on paper," Daisy is saying. "The first things that come to mind. They might be images, like mountains or stars. Or maybe feeling words. Or anything! Doesn't matter. Just write them down."

My words are pretty predictable:

*Home*

*Music*

*Art*

*Diamonds*

Sally writes:

*Mouse*

I'm racking my brain for less predictable words, then realize I'm not supposed to try too hard. That defeats the point.

So I add:

*Charcoal*

*Rain*

*Summer*

Not sure why. But hey.

Daisy has her hands behind her back and is leaning over our piece of paper. She starts humming, then sings, "Charcoal rain, take me away. Lost on summer. No way I'm making it."

I stare at her. Her voice is amazing. And those words. Wow. Billie would be impressed. I notice Sparrow is also looking over. *Yeah, Sparrow. There's someone else at Curlew Point who can sing!*

"That's um, really good," I say.

Daisy shrugs. "They're your words!" She moves on to another group.

Later, when we have to write our own lyrics, it's hard to get Daisy's lyrics out of my head. Also, her voice. So warm and salty. Like balmy summer evenings.

Finally, I get to:

*Feeling the pain. The summer rain. Paint me black, charcoal. Take me back home.*

Sally looks impressed. I see definite evidence of her mouse squiggling in her skort pocket and look away quickly so no one else sees what I see. I hate seeing Sally getting teased.

## seven

**I DO MY USUAL COVID SAFETY ROUTINE** at the Diamonds reception desk. Temperature check. Hand sanitizer. I scribble my initials next to my name, which is now printed in the logbook. I can't help feeling a bit pleased about this. Something about seeing my name printed in full makes me feel very welcome at Diamonds.

I could go and hang out by myself in John Johnson's unit. But I still can't shake the feeling that John Johnson's ghost is watching me. When I tune Dad's guitar and try a few chords, I don't get the happy vibes that music usually gives me.

I wander through the grounds and through the main building, looking for Mum. I don't find Mum. But I find Meg in the office. She beams when she sees me.

"How y'all settling in?" she says, motioning to the gray cushioned seat on the other side of the desk. I plonk myself down.

"It's all right," I say.

"It's lovely having someone young around. Keeps the older people young, you know. And not a lot of them get regular visitors. Especially since all this COVID stuff. We have to be extra cautious. Many of them have family out of state who can't travel. Tragic, if you ask me."

I nod. I hadn't thought about this side of the pandemic. For me, lockdown was a breeze. I got to hang out in my room all day every day. Betsy would pop in and check on me if Mum was on shift. And if Mum wasn't on shift, she and I watched rom-com after rom-com. Before COVID, Mum had a strict one-movie-a-week policy because she was frightened about me getting square eyes or something. During lockdown, Mum let go of all previous policies and I got to watch movies every day.

But for people at Diamonds, things would have been really different. I am realizing that now. They wouldn't have been able to see anyone, because they were most at risk of getting sick from COVID.

"You know, you could help me out with the activities, if you're looking for an afternoon activity," says Meg. "It's choir practice this afternoon. You like singing, right?"

Sure, I like singing. In the privacy of my own room.

But something about Meg's warm tone, and the thought of all these poor lonely old people without families, makes me say "Yes."

Meg looks like she's going to explode with happiness. "That's amazing!" she says, beaming. "I absolutely loathe singing. I sound like a drunk walrus. How do you feel about taking over the choir while you're here? Leading the residents in a bit of a sing-along?"

"Um . . ." I look down at my lap. A sing-along? I am really regretting ever stepping into this office.

"Come, I'll show you the ropes. The troops will be gathering in the garden as we speak. Funny story— folks aren't supposed to sing indoors right now because of all this COVID business. But we figure a garden choir works."

There are about twenty older people milling around in the bandstand when we enter. I am relieved to see a familiar face—Audrey. She motions me over.

"Get this. They want us to sing 'On a Bicycle Built for Two,'" says Audrey. "Can you believe it?"

"What's that? I've never heard of it," I say.

"Of course you haven't," says Audrey. "That's because you're not seventy-five! God help me, Queenie. Singing this rubbish makes me feel like rolling into an early grave."

"Don't say that, Audrey!" I protest.

"Right!" says Meg, clapping to get everyone's attention. "Good news! Our lovely young Queenie has offered to lead the sing-along this afternoon. Queenie, this is Jerry, our pianist. He can play anything your heart desires. Can't you, Jerry?"

Someone's set up a keyboard in the bandstand. Jerry sits on the piano stool, smiling at us all. He's gray-haired but definitely younger than most people in the crowd. I wonder if he's a resident or is brought in especially for choir sessions.

The residents turn to look at me. Most are smiling encouragingly. I can't believe I am in this situation. I would love for the ground to open and swallow me up.

"Okay, great! I'll leave you to it!" Meg strides off across the grounds.

I clear my throat, hoping words or anything useful will cough itself into existence. I turn to Audrey. She nods at me encouragingly. She must have picked up on my stage fright, because she speaks for me.

"Queenie is going to shake things up a bit. Give us a taste of something new and fresh. Aren't you, Queenie?"

A few residents clap politely. I recognize toothless Duncan in the back row, nodding furiously.

"Well?" says Audrey. "What's your favorite song, Queenie? Show us how it goes."

"Ah, it's called 'Ocean Eyes,' but I don't think—"

"Jerry, 'Ocean Eyes'! Hit it!" yells Audrey. Thank goodness she knows how to control a situation.

Jerry, the guy who can play anything your heart desires, is fumbling with his phone. He glances up at me, uncertain. But he puts the phone on the piano and starts playing some notes. By Jove, he's got it. The guy really can play anything.

I let the first few verses play out. Everyone's eyes are on me.

Finally, I start singing. My voice sounds like a feather. But gets louder. I notice Audrey smiling at me.

By the end of the second chorus, I am at full volume. I am actually enjoying myself. Where was this confidence a week ago, when I was waiting to go on the stage at Curlew Point in front of the whole school?

Audrey whoops and everyone claps and cheers when I am done.

"Right," I say. "Jerry—from the top."

I take the Diamonds choir through each verse. Slowly. Tediously. It's like teaching a tractor how to walk. But we get there after half an hour or so. I see Meg watching me from her office window, a grin on her face.

o o o

I feel like I'm floating as I push Audrey down the path, toward her unit. I've never in my life done anything like that.

I hang out with Audrey for a bit, doing a crossword puzzle. I notice she wears a wedding ring.

"Are you married?" I ask. She's never mentioned a husband.

"I was," she says. "A long time ago. Rupert. Lovely fella."

She fills in 14 across.

"So you've been alone awhile?" I ask.

"Thirty years," she says.

Thirty years? I can't even comprehend that. That's nearly all of Mum's life.

"Oh," I say.

She shrugs. "It's fine. We had a lovely romance for about twenty years. No kids. Just us, gallivanting around the world. We did loads of traveling." She sighs. "What about you?" she says. "Any boys?" She's waggling her eyebrows in a very disconcerting way.

"Blugh," I say. "No way."

There is one boy. Dory. I've noticed him a few times now. I don't know what it is. He looks older than the other boys. Like he should be at the upper school. And there's something about the way he just does his own thing. Sits on his own at lunch, playing chess against himself. He doesn't care when the other kids jeer at him. He just shrugs it off. It's kinda cool.

"And you've got lots of friends?" asks Audrey.

"Nah," I say.

I feel Audrey's eyes on me. She's waiting for me to elaborate.

"I don't know," I say, filling in 7 down: *victory*. "I don't mind my own company. Ever since Sparrow ditched me."

"Okay, back up—who's this Sparrow girl, and why would she ditch a kid like you? Is she nuts?"

I grin. "Nuts as a pecan pie! Apparently, she could sing better than me. I don't know exactly what happened. We just grew apart, I suppose."

Audrey is doing air punches, her thin arms quavering. "If I ever meet this Sparrow girl, I'll—bop, bop!" She makes to punch imaginary Sparrow in the nose.

I giggle.

## eight

**AUDREY AND I HAVE BEEN HANGING OUT** every afternoon. As well as choir, Meg's roped me in for Craft-a-noon Wednesday and cooking lessons on Thursday.

"I love that you're getting Audrey inspired again," says Meg one night at dinner. "She was all mopey before you arrived."

After cooking class that Thursday, I walk right into a dining room feud. Two residents are yelling at each other from across the room. I bring my homework beside Audrey, who's got an unfilled crossword on her lap and is gazing gleefully at the battle.

"What's happened?" I ask.

"Well," says Audrey, cracking her knuckles, "Maud has Alzheimer's, which means she gets confused sometimes.

And Maud is accusing Ron of taking her handbag from her place. Ron swears he's never even been inside her unit. Anyway, *ouch*!" We both flinch as Maud whacks Ron really hard across the face with what seems to be her handbag. Ron roars in pain.

One of the caregivers bolts to the scene and steps between Maud and Ron. Brave guy. Maud looks like she's about to strike again. But the caregiver's firm, calm tones seem to do the trick. Maud slinks back to her chair. Ron huffs and storms out of the room.

"Bet you never got this kind of entertainment back home," says Audrey.

"If I'm honest, no. I didn't. It was just me and Mum. And our neighbor, Betsy. But she's no Maud, that's for sure."

Walter wanders in, singing a Frank Sinatra song I recognize from a play Mum and I saw together before COVID. His tighty-whities are pulled up to his rib cage.

I love this guy. He's so *himself*.

It takes me a moment to realize Audrey's cheeks are flaming red. She's looking down in her lap. This isn't the Audrey I've come to know over the last week.

I prod her knee.

"Is everything okay?" I ask.

"Yep," she mutters. She glances at Walter, who is looking over at us, grinning. Audrey turns a deeper shade of cadmium red.

"Uh-oh. You like him, don't you?" I whisper. "You like Walter."

Audrey can't look me in the eyes. She's shaking her head. What happened to *I could date a ski instructor*? Audrey looks all kinds of nervous. It's pretty sweet.

I've seen enough rom-coms to know that Audrey most definitely has the hots for Walter.

And the way Walter is gazing over at us intermittently? I am guessing he has the hots for Audrey.

I feel like I need to do something about this.

I wheel Audrey to her unit because she has some urgent British soap opera she has to get back for. Nothing to do with Walter, she pinkie-swears.

I sit through the corny show, watching Audrey. When it's done, she turns her wheelchair to face me.

"Yes, Queenie?" she says. "What is it?"

"Just wondering why you don't just tell Walter you like him, which you clearly do. It's like Birdie, from that show you were just watching. Look how happy she was when she finally had the guts to say how she felt about Harry."

Audrey groans and turns away from me.

"Queenie? You know what? Things are complicated. Life is complicated. You're twelve, so I wouldn't expect you to understand."

I dodge in front of her so she can't avoid me. "Actually, I do understand. It's easy. Walter likes you. I can see it in his face. The way he was looking over at you tonight. Ask him out for dinner or something."

She scoffs. "Ha!"

"Why not?" I say.

She narrows her eyes at me. At first I think she's annoyed. But then I realize she's just thinking.

"I can't, because he might say no. It's been thirty years, Queenie! Rejection might be the death of me!"

"I doubt it," I say. Audrey might be ninety-three, but she's buff, and amazing. She looks like she's going to live forever.

Audrey has clearly had enough of the conversation, because she's channel surfing and doing her best to ignore me again.

Back in John Johnson's unit, Garfield listens as I try putting the lyrics I wrote in Daisy's class to Dad's guitar again. I've been tinkering around with a few different chord progressions. But tonight, the tune literally gives me tingles.

*Feeling the pain. The summer rain.*

*Paint me black, charcoal. Take me back home.*

*Faded and gray, we will all move away.*

*All move away, on a long summer's day.*

I sing so softly, I swear it's just me and the world.

"Love that," says Mum from the doorway.

"I thought you were on shift," I say. I feel my cheeks redden.

"I am. Just had to grab something." She jiggles her name tag and darts into the hall. "As you were, Queenie Pants!" she calls over her shoulder.

I sigh and put the guitar back on its stand.

## nine

**MUM MEETS ME AT THE BUS STOP THE NEXT DAY.** She's waving her phone around.

"Guess what, Queenie! I found us a place! You're going to love it."

Mum says we can drive by it. We'll have to come back for the open house tomorrow. In the car, I scroll through pictures on the real estate app, gazing lovingly at the little Queenslander on Pickle Street. I see myself sometime in the near future ensconced in the biggest room, on the window seat, making music.

"Gosh, the location's perfect," says Mum, turning into the cul-de-sac. "You can get the bus straight to school from here. And it's only a ten-minute drive to Diamonds!"

The Queenslander (which I've already named Pearl) is perched on a hill. A poinciana tree shades the whole front garden. The tree is laden with flaming-red flowers. Even though the house looks like it needs a paint job and is leaning a bit, it's so perfect I could cry. I almost don't miss our old house for a moment.

"Let's move in immediately," I say.

"Wouldn't that be good!" Mum waves her crossed fingers at me. "We have to hope for the best, Queenie Pants. It's a tough market out there."

Mum treats us to burgers at Miro's. We sit side by side in one of the red booths. A good-looking waiter with surf hair comes to take our order. He spends way too long chatting and laughing with Mum. Her eyes are doing the twinkly thing.

I frown at her.

"What?" she says, all innocent-like, when the guy walks away.

"You like him," I say.

Mum laughs. "Hardly! I don't even know the poor guy!"

"His name is Jake," I say. "It says it on his badge."

"Anyway," says Mum, changing the subject. "I read about the end-of-year concert in the newsletter. You didn't tell me! I would have come, silly!"

"Why? It was pretty dumb," I say. Sparrow immediately springs into my head, warming my neural pathways with her delicious tones. Darn you, Sparrow Hawkins.

"You played, didn't you?" asks Mum.

I cringe. Shake my head. Stare at the turquoise laminate tabletop.

"Queenie Pants?" says Mum, lifting my chin and forcing me to make eye contact. "I thought you were practicing 'Ocean Eyes' for the concert. You worked so hard on that."

I avert my gaze and shake my head. Luckily, Jake bounces back with a basket of fries, which makes Mum giddy, and takes her attention away from me.

The truth is, I'm still trying to process why I couldn't walk onstage after Sparrow. Of course I couldn't have played "Ocean Eyes." Sparrow had literally just played it, seconds before me. And she sounded a million times better than I ever could. I could have played my other favorite song, "Time," by Tom Waits. I know it like the back of my hand.

But walking away was so easy.

"Beet burger?" says Jake. I nod and take a bite. Beet juice drips down my chin. Mum smiles and mops me up. She sometimes has a knack for making me feel like an oversize toddler.

The Frank Sinatra song Walter was singing yesterday comes on the radio. I hold my burger, listening. An idea is forming.

What if . . . ? Oh, man, it would be so cute. What if Audrey serenaded Walter with this song? I've heard her sing in choir. She's pretty good!

"What are you grinning at?" says Mum.

"It's a nice song," I say.

*o o o*

Later, I swing past Audrey's unit to see if she's still up.

Audrey's out of her wheelchair, propped up in bed with loads of pillows. She grins as I push open the door.

I start singing Frank Sinatra from the doorway. "What is this?" asks Audrey. "A singing telegram service?"

I laugh. "No! I am serenading you."

"Charming," says Audrey. "Keep going, then."

She lies back on her pillows and closes her eyes. I sing the whole song from the end of her bed, reading the lyrics on Mum's phone.

"So?" I ask. "How do you feel?"

"Perfectly charmed."

"Exactly!" I say.

She opens one eye and studies me.

"You are going to serenade Walter. It's been decided."

"Has it, now?" says Audrey. "And who decided that?"

"I did," I say. I know my grin is smug. But I can't wipe it away. "You told me you can't tell Walter how you feel. But you can sing it. And Walter likes Sinatra. He's always singing Sinatra."

A bit of me expects Audrey to laugh me down. So I am surprised when Audrey's mouth twists. I can see she is considering the proposition.

"So, if I were to . . . How? How would this work exactly? Do I just come up to him and start singing at him?"

I chuckle. That could be fun. But it could also be fun to do things properly.

"It's the Christmas concert next week, right? Now that I am officially choir leader, I can make sure you get a spot when you can sing to Walter. The PA system will be all set up. Walter will be there. It'll be perfect."

Audrey's eyes are still narrowed. But a smile passes her lips. Helping Audrey serenade Walter is the best idea I've had all year, even if I do say so myself. I give myself an invisible pat on the back.

## ten

**I'VE NEVER BEEN TO AN OPEN HOUSE BEFORE.** Why would I have? Open houses are for people who need homes. And until a couple of weeks ago, I was not one of those people.

Now, it turns out, I am.

I am standing on the lawn with about sixty other people, in front of the Queenslander Mum and I drove past yesterday.

"COVID policy means we can only let five groups through at a time," says the blond real estate agent on the porch. She's talking to a pregnant woman who has three small kids with her. "Also, we need you all to sanitize and wear face masks."

"I have to get to the next open house, though," says the woman. "It's over in twenty minutes. Just let us through quickly. Please. We won't touch anything. You know what? The kids can wait outside."

"Sorry. It's against policy. You are just going to have to wait like everyone else." The mother sighs dramatically, then pulls the kids with her as they march down the hill.

I glance at Mum. She's sucking the end of her ponytail and scratching her eczema. Uh-oh. Pregnant lady is not the only one feeling the heat.

Speaking of which, it is about a million degrees. Sweat is trickling down my back. I wish I'd worn a cotton tank instead of this synthetic cowgirl shirt I found at the thrift shop.

We form a kind of a line. There's no social distancing. I feel like we are jelly beans trying to squeeze into a jar. Kids are crying. Couples are bickering. I put my ear to the conversation behind me.

"This is nothing. You should have seen the last open house I went to," says a girl. "I swear there was like a hundred people! The agent told me not to bother applying. Said they wouldn't consider an hourly worker."

"At least you have a job," says the guy she's talking to. "Try being unemployed. If it wasn't for Freddie's mum,

I'd be getting out of this area. You know the surf's just as good down near Ryans Head? Maybe better. And what about that woman? She brought her dog. Is she crazy?"

"I just wish I could buy my own place," says the girl. "You gotta be a home owner. The rental market sucks."

"Totally," agrees the guy.

I squeeze Mum's hand. Partly to reassure her. Partly to stop her from scratching her eczema.

I'd never thought Mum being an hourly worker was a bad thing. Until right now.

I'd also never thought about needing to own our own home. Mum says we have savings. But it's for if her car breaks down. And maybe a trip if we can ever travel again after the pandemic. I don't think it's enough to buy a whole house.

We finally get inside. On closer inspection, Pearl isn't so much rustic-cute as falling apart. The stove looks like it's a million years old. We overhear the male real estate agent telling a family that two of the three burners don't work.

"Oh, hi, Dimitri!" calls Mum when he's finished chatting.

"Hey, Clare!" The Dimitri guy pushes down his face mask momentarily and grins at Mum. His teeth are very white.

53

"You know each other?" I say.

"Dimitri sold Betsy's place," says Mum.

Traitor. I narrow my eyes at him. Mum catches me and subtly elbows me in the ribs.

"You're in rentals now?" Mum asks Dimitri.

"Yeah! Sales are nuts right now. I needed to step out for a breather. Can't say rentals are much easier. You've probably guessed that, though. Angie and I are literally swimming in applications." He nods toward the line at the front door.

"Bananas," says Mum. "Do you have anything else coming on the market?"

"There are things. But they don't hang around long!" says Dimitri.

Dimitri's skin is so glossy. I imagine the factory where real estate agents are made. It's clean and shiny and made of metal.

I leave Mum chatting with Real Estate Dimitri and go on my own personal tour of my future house. The good thing about Mum being chummy with the real estate agent is that we might have half a chance of getting it.

I stand in the doorway of one of the bedrooms. It's the one in the picture. My room, theoretically. The walls are peachy, which is a good sign.

But it's not my old room. Not even close.

The real estate lady guarding the front door pipes up from down the hall. "If everyone could make their way out of the house, that'd be great!" she says. "We have quite a few people to come through today! Thank you for your cooperation. Enjoy your day!"

She's way too cheery.

"See ya!" Mum calls to Dimitri, who waves to Mum like she's family.

I feel drained on the car trip home, like someone just emptied me out. Mum says a few nice things about the house but gives up when I don't reply.

I play my Billie playlist on Spotify to distract myself from my rumbling tummy and all those applications for the Queenslander. I find myself looking forward to hanging out with Audrey and the gang, prodding wannabe food and imagining I can live in an old people's village for the rest of my life.

## eleven

**AUDREY AND I ARE OUT** in the Diamond Sands band-stand later that day. I can't believe it's possible that the day has managed to heat up even more. But there's a slight breeze out here, under the tropical birch.

"Pretend I'm Walter. Now, sing," I say. I am sitting on the grass. Audrey is on the stage.

Audrey clears her throat, closes her eyes, and sings a verse of Sinatra. She's shaky and her voice is swallowed up by the breeze. But she gets through the whole song.

"That's pretty good!" I say, clapping. "Love it."

"It sucked," says Audrey. Should old people even know that word?

"It didn't suck. You just need to project your voice. Sing to the back of the room. Or garden. You know."

Audrey rolls her eyes. She clears her throat again. This time, her voice cracks with effort. She drops the imaginary mic.

"It's useless, Queenie. I'm useless."

"So don't do it, then. No one is making you."

I think of that terrible moment, wavering in the wings. Staring out at the whole school. All those blank faces.

Then walking away.

Not doing things is easy. Right?

Audrey sighs and holds the imaginary mic to her mouth again. "Fine. I'm doing it," she says.

Audrey gets better with every lap of the song. After five takes, though, I am done. Sweat has soaked my shirt, and I am gagging for a drink.

I wheel Audrey through the garden. We spot Walter in the distance, sitting among the roses in his undies. A book in his lap. His eyes closed. Audrey quickly looks away.

As we roll up the avenue, I stop.

"Was wondering if I'd bump into you," says Sparrow Hawkins.

She sits on a bench, next to Neville Hawkins. Neville must be her grandfather, judging by the look of them both. And the last name.

I hang my head. Sparrow surrounds me at school. Now she's crowding me here. My home—for all intents and purposes.

"Are you going to introduce me?" says Audrey, tugging my hand.

"Audrey, Sparrow. Sparrow, Audrey."

"Ahhhh," says Audrey, with way too much inflection. "The famous Sparrow Hawkins." She rolls toward Sparrow. Sparrow shoots me a look.

"Famous, huh? Good famous or bad famous?" she says.

"Let's just say you are a favorite topic of conversation for Queenie and me."

I could die. I could literally die right now. I know it would be unexpected, given that I am the youngest person here, other than Sparrow, by like decades. But I'd be happy to let the soil take me whole.

Sparrow, on the other hand, looks very fascinated with this turn of events.

"Well, you're famous, too, Audrey," says Sparrow, too sweet and sticky for my liking. "My granddad has the hots for you."

"He does, does he?" says Audrey. I can see her looking at Neville as if for the first time.

Of course. Another love interest. But then, Audrey is

pretty spunky. For some reason, though, Audrey's only got eyes for Walter.

"I saw you practicing in the bandstand," says Sparrow. "Are you rehearsing for the Christmas concert next week? Granddad's asked if I could come in and sing something. 'Course I'm going to. It'll be so fun!"

I groan. Audrey shoots me a knowing look.

Of course she's going to. Why wouldn't she? Any opportunity to upstage Queenie Jean Anderson. And here I was under the delusion that Diamonds was *my* thing.

I give Sparrow the dirtiest look I can summon. I want her to understand how unwelcome she is at the Christmas concert. How unwelcome she is at Diamonds period. She stole my song at the end-of-year school concert. And now she's going to steal my thunder from the Diamonds Christmas concert.

My dislike for Sparrow knows no limitations.

"What about you, Queenie?" says Sparrow. I know she's smirking. Yes, she's definitely smirking.

"Queenie's our choir leader, so she doesn't have a choice," says Audrey defensively.

Something about the way Sparrow's eyebrows go up to meet her braids makes me think Audrey might have put her off-kilter. I won't lie. I quite like this.

## twelve

**"ANY WORD ABOUT THE HOUSE?"** I ask Mum the next day.

We're sitting on John Johnson's bed. She's braiding my hair. This is the number one thing I love about weekends. Time with Mum—just her and me. Later, Mum is taking me to the art gallery. There's a portrait exhibition on, apparently. We haven't been to the art gallery since before COVID. In fact, we haven't done any of that stuff, like going to the movies or the theater.

"Nope. No word," says Mum. "Hold still."

"Ouch! You're pulling."

"Sorry," she mutters, the hairband between her teeth. She spits it out so she can talk. "Dimitri and I have been texting, though."

"Dimitri?" I say, stunned. "Real Estate Dimitri?"

"Yep. Real Estate Dimitri."

I grimace.

We sit in silence for a bit while I process this information. Then I ask, "You're texting about the house, right? That's a good sign. Dimitri said there were hundreds of applications. If he's texting you, we must be in with a good chance."

"Hm," says Mum. I don't know what that means. "I'm sure it all helps."

I don't *love* that Mum is texting some random guy. So it's a relief that the guy is just Dimitri the real estate guy. The guy who is definitely going to get us Pearl the flaky house.

If Dimitri had been some other guy—well.

Mum's not into dating, which suits me perfectly. I have always been so glad Sarah hasn't ever gotten through to Mum about the wonders of Tinder and e-Romance or whatever rubbish floats Sarah's boat.

Mum's an independent lady. She doesn't need all that.

Anyway, she has me.

o o o

The portrait exhibition is fun. Not all twelve-year-olds love schlepping around art galleries on their weekend.

But this is just what me and Mum do. We schlep. We've been schlepping around art galleries and going to movies and the theater for years. Because of this, I have an unusual appreciation for art and other grown-up things.

For example, I really like these moody charcoal portraits of people on trains. The artist has drawn them without the people knowing they're being drawn, which seems a bit creepy. But the portraits are fascinating.

I zone in on one of a homeless couple sitting forehead to forehead on the train, a milk bottle between them. All their belongings at their feet.

I feel so sad for the couple. It must be awful not having a home.

It takes me a few beats to realize that homelessness comes in lots of shades. Sometimes, it's you and your whole life in bags on a train. Sometimes, it's helping ninety-three-year-olds to find the words they need to serenade the man of their dreams.

# thirteen

"**AH, QUEENIE, THERE YOU ARE,**" says Mr. Grey, stopping me in the hall later that week. My heart sinks. Stress leave must be over. Which means Daisy is no longer our music teacher.

Mr. Grey doesn't look much less stressed than before his leave. His shirt is still buttoned up tight on his neck. His bald head shines like a light bulb. His mouth is pursed in a tight little bunch, as if he's just sucked a lemon dry.

"You didn't play at the concert," says Mr. Grey.

Great. Here we go.

"Nope," I say. "The guitar was out of tune. Also, Sparrow played my song."

Mr. Grey frowns. "If the guitar was out of tune, you could have tuned it. So what if Sparrow played your song? You could have played another one."

"I couldn't have, Mr. Grey."

Mr. Grey shakes his head. "You know you're very good at guitar, Queenie. Better than most kids your age. I don't know what it's going to take to get you to play in front of people. I thought you'd made a breakthrough this year."

I look at Mr. Grey's shoes. They are also very shiny. I can see myself.

"Well, I am disappointed that I went to all that trouble to include your name on the poster, and you couldn't even be bothered to show up," says Mr. Grey. He marches off down the hall.

Antarctica ripples through me, fanning out, taking over. He doesn't get that I did show up. Well, almost. The stage wings count, right?

Still. I can't help feeling like Mr. Grey isn't being unreasonable.

o o o

"I'm going to perform at the Christmas concert," I tell Audrey that afternoon at our secret rehearsal. I know once I tell her, I can't chicken out. Now that the words are out, though, I am pretty sure I made a big fat mistake.

"Do what at the Christmas concert?" says Audrey, clearly not listening. She's fussing around with the CD player again. I can see from over here that the CD is in the wrong way. I reach over and flip it for her.

"Sing a song."

"Congratulations," says Audrey. "You and me both. What are you going to sing?"

"Not sure. It has to be pretty obscure. Otherwise Sparrow might sing the same song. She has a history of doing that."

"You should sing something really traditional. Like 'Silent Night.' Sparrow won't expect that."

Audrey is a genius. Yes. I can already play "Silent Night." This will be a cinch. There's no way I will be able to chicken out.

"What inspired all this, then?" she asks. "Heading up the choir not enough for you, hm?"

I know it sounds corny. But I'm going to say it anyway. "I'm inspired by you, actually. If you can get up there in front of everyone and serenade Walter, I can freaking get up there and serenade all you lovely people. You've inspired me, Audrey."

She blushes. But then waves me away. "Oh, be quiet. I couldn't inspire a goldfish to swim laps in a fish bowl. That's called blowing smoke up my bum, Queenie. And I don't like it."

She says that, but I can see clearly that she does like it. She likes it a lot.

## fourteen

**"WEAR THIS ONE," I SAY TO MUM** when she gets out of the shower. It's the morning of the concert. I'm holding up her yellow polka-dot dress.

"Is it Christmassy enough?" she says, holding it against her body and twirling.

"Yep!" I say. "It's cheery."

"You look cheery," she says, smiling. "Love the reindeer."

Audrey and I have matching T-shirts, which we have cross-stitched with reindeer. Mine's pretty wonky, because I have never cross-stitched before. But it's cute. Kitschy cute.

Mum and I sweep across the garden, arm in arm. My stomach jolts when I see Sparrow, of all people, standing on a chair, hanging streamers from the bandstand beams. That's supposed to be my job. This is my place. Not Sparrow's.

"Hey, Queenie!" she says.

I wait for a spiky comment to follow. It doesn't come.

"Wanna help?" she asks, holding out a streamer. "Thought I'd brighten things up a bit. Granddad is always complaining how dull things are around here."

And there it is. The comment that we've all been waiting for.

"I'm good," I say. I leave Mum chatting with Meg and go to find Audrey.

Audrey's unit is locked, which is unusual. I knock a few times. Finally, I hear noises. Her face appears in the gap of the door.

"Oh, blimey. It's just you. Come in, Queenie."

I watch Audrey's arms quaver as she pins her thin hair to the top of her head.

"Let me do that for you," I say. I notice her breathing is shallow.

"I'm fine," she says.

"You don't look too fine. You're pale. Do you feel okay?"

She closes her eyes. The dread pulls at my tummy. What if Audrey is dying? But then something occurs to me.

"You're nervous, aren't you? About the concert."

She nods and looks relieved that I've put words to the experience.

"I'm freaking terrified, Queenie," she says.

"You're going to be amazing," I say. "Just like we practiced. Imagine you're singing with the whole choir."

o o o

I would never tell her, but Sparrow has done a pretty amazing job with the bandstand. It's decorated with every color under the sun. Streamers hang from every beam. The whole thing sparkles.

Nora and a few other residents wear reindeer ears. Walter is fully dressed in a three-piece woolen suit. I can't believe the guy can go from undies to woolen suit in the middle of summer. This concert must mean a lot to him.

It's a bit before eleven, so friends and family are strolling across the garden, greeting their older relatives with a light kiss. Some bring flowers. There are kids and grown-ups and all sorts of people. I recognize Sparrow's mum among them. I haven't seen her since I used to go on playdates at the Hawkinses' house. I wave, but she must not recognize me, because she turns away. The day care center kids walk in, in two wobbly rows, holding hands. They're wearing reindeer ears with bells, and Santa T-shirts. They are so cute and small. They plonk down in front of the roses.

Meg greets everyone in her usual messy, warm way. Huge arms making us all feel hugged.

The concert starts with the day care kids forming a cluster on the bandstand stage. They sing "Jingle Bells," accompanied by Jerry. Even though the kids are totally off-key, I could eat them up, they are so sweet and squeaky.

Nora does an old-fashioned number I don't recognize. Her voice quavers, but she plays the keyboard well.

Wayne sings "Little Drummer Boy" a cappella, which is pretty moving.

When Meg signals, I lead the Diamonds choir up to the front of the room. There's shuffling and bumping. Jerry sets himself up on the keyboard.

I stand in front of the choir, like a choirmaster, holding my imaginary baton. Every eye is on me.

Jerry plays the intro to "Ocean Eyes," and I count in the choir.

They sound awful. Mainly because we've been trying out harmonies, and well, let's just say, harmonies were a bit advanced for this group.

But we make it through the song. The crowd claps politely. When we sit on plastic chairs set up on the lawn, I catch Sparrow looking over at me. Her look is hard to read.

"We have a couple more acts," says Meg. She studies the set list I gave her. "This one is by . . . Anonymous."

Audrey rolls down the path toward the bandstand. She wheels up the ramp.

I've prepped Jerry, so as soon as Audrey touches the mic, he launches in with the intro to "The Way You Look Tonight," the Sinatra song Walter likes.

I'm grateful that Jerry doesn't give Audrey an opportunity to back out of this.

Audrey holds the mic with both hands and presses it to her lips. Even from back here, I can see she's nervous. She's making me nervous. It's like her nerves are stretching through the lawn and coming up through the soles of my feet.

I notice Walter sitting up straighter, a grin spread across his face, which is 100 percent turned in Audrey's direction.

A verse passes without a word. Audrey's hands are shaking. She stares soundlessly out at the audience. At Walter. Jerry carries on, oblivious.

Audrey is tanking. I can't let this happen. Not after all our afternoons of hard work.

I make my way through the plastic chairs and crouch as close to Audrey as I can. I hold her quaking hands in mine.

Under my firm grip, the shaking slows. I feel her whole body relax beside me. I start singing softly. After a line or two, she joins in. I see Mum push tears away from her eyes. Meg, too, looks like she's blubbing up and trying really hard not to.

Most of the residents have all eyes on us. (Except Nora, who's snoring loudly.)

Walter stares at Audrey the whole time. He stands at some point and drifts through the crowd toward the bandstand. Toward Audrey.

"For you, Walter," croaks Audrey when the song is done. Her blush is flying off the Richter scale.

Walter lifts her hand to his mouth and kisses it. Meg and Mum and a few residents applaud loudly. Meg wolf whistles.

I am grinning so hard it hurts. Could Audrey and Walter be more sweet if they tried?

"Thank you, Queenie," Audrey whispers. But she's still holding the mic, so everyone hears it.

"Shall we?" says Walter. He pushes Audrey's chair so she can sit next to him.

Meg doesn't even get the chance to introduce the next act, because Sparrow is already standing onstage, beaming out at us like she's a headlight.

"Today, I will be singing 'Silent Night,' my absolute favorite Christmas carol of all time."

I groan audibly. I try to catch Audrey's eye. But Audrey's only got eyes for one person. And it's not me.

I slip across the lawn just as the first few notes of Sparrow's delicious voice threaten to melt my heart.

Well done, Queenie, well done. You've let yourself down like a lead balloon.

## fifteen

**SINCE IT'S THE LAST WEEK OF SCHOOL** for the year, the teachers are all about Christmas movies and YouTube. Mr. Baqri sets up a slip-and-slide on the lawn this afternoon, and we're all allowed to slide down in our school uniforms. He hands out ice pops to all the kids afterward. It's the best.

I can see Mum's cheeriness is dialed up when she meets me at the bus stop after school.

"We didn't get the house you loved," says Mum.

"Wait, what? I thought Dimitri was all over it? Isn't that what you've been texting about?"

Mum's still smiling, trying to be cheery. "Dimitri says we had a strong application, but the owners chose a professional couple from Sydney," says Mum.

We walk three blocks toward Diamonds. The sun bakes my school shirt, which has well and truly dried out again after the slip-and-slide.

I don't talk. I'm processing what this means. We lost Peachy. Now we've lost Pearl. Mum and I seem to be unlucky in the housing department.

But then, living at Diamonds is kind of awesome. I've befriended Audrey and helped her and Walter get together. I'm a choir leader now.

"Are you okay, Queenie?" Mum says eventually.

"I don't care about the house," I say. "Really. It's actually fine."

"What do you mean you don't care? I thought that house was everything you'd ever wanted."

"I mean, I want to stay at Diamonds."

"Ah, Queenie." Mum squeezes the top of my arm. She wants me to stop.

"Mum? What's the matter?"

"I love that you love Diamonds. But Sue needs our unit. Mrs. Lim is moving in on Wednesday."

"Wednesday?" I splutter. "But that's two days away! What about Audrey?"

"Audrey will keep kicking along. You can visit her whenever you like. She'd love that."

"But what about us?" Sue and the guy at the open

house's comments are running through my mind like the Metro train. "Are we going to be homeless?"

Mum plasters on her grin. We are at the Diamonds reception desk now and start our COVID safety routine.

"Sarah emailed and says she knows a place we can stay for a bit. She's sent me the lady's details. I was going to call this afternoon," says Mum. "Everything will be fine, Queenie. I promise."

o o o

After I've packed, Mum says I can go say goodbye to Audrey. She's not in the dining room or hanging around reception, giving the receptionist a hard time for not ordering her cheesecake from the bakery for dessert. She's not sitting out on the common room porch, catching the afternoon sun. Duncan is. He raises his hand and grins at me. His grin is both toothy and toothless at the same time. It's quite an achievement.

"How was school?" he asks.

"So-so," I say. "We're leaving tonight, you know."

"Oh," says Duncan, his face long. "That's a pity. It was nice having some young blood around for a change. It's been a lonely year."

I put my hand on Duncan's shoulder. Being this close to him, I notice he smells like toffee.

Meg's in her office, her clunky shoes on her desk, a pen in her big bun. She's on the phone. I step back, cautious not to intrude on a private conversation. But I realize she's just ordering pizza. She waves me in. As soon as the phone's down, she drops her feet and leans forward on her elbows.

"So you cats are off, hey?" she says. "You found a nice house you like?"

"Nah," I say.

"What, you don't like the house? Or you haven't found one? Where are you going to live?"

"We haven't found one yet. We're going to stay with a friend of a friend's. The Elliots."

The truth is, the Elliots aren't Sarah's friends as such. Sarah's friend's neighbor heard there was a family looking to share for a bit to cover their rent, because the dad lost his job during COVID. When I quizzed Mum for more, she didn't know anything about the Elliots, which seems like a very dicey living arrangement. We could be living with a family of axe murderers come tonight.

When Meg nods compassionately, her pen slides out of her bun and clatters on the desk.

"Well, you come back and visit us," says Meg.

I bite my cheek and nod. Before I can change my mind, I lean across the desk and hug Meg. She squeezes me back.

I knock a few times on unit 119—Audrey's place. There's no answer. I'm about to give up when I hear shuffling. A voice follows.

I push open the door and peer into the darkness.

"Audrey?"

Audrey's in there. So is Walter. They're sitting in bed together watching a movie on a laptop. I guess it's Walter's, since Audrey has an aversion to technology. The computer light makes their faces glow purple.

I'm about to slip away so I don't disturb them.

"Queenie?" croaks Audrey, seeing me. "You're not sneaking off, are you, without saying goodbye?"

Tears are streaming down Audrey's cheeks. Down Walter's, too. But the tears aren't for me.

"Sally just kissed Harry. Finally," says Audrey, pointing to the laptop.

I'm going to miss it here.

*the second move*

# CHESS WIZARD

## sixteen

MUM'S DATSUN PUTTS DOWN SENTIMENTAL AVENUE—
a leafy street I've never been down before in my life. The
houses are small and squished together. They're all on
stilts. It must flood here sometimes.

When Dory opens the door of 16 Sentimental Avenue,
I suddenly realize that I do know who the Elliots are.

My throat constricts.

Dory's the only kid at school taller than me. By a
good head of hair.

"Chess wizard," I say under my breath.

"Cool girl," says Dory in reply. He's smiling.

This takes me by surprise. Cool girl? Hardly.
Chipmunk girl with chronic stage fright. Not cool. Not
very cool at all.

I really hope I'm not blushing too badly.

"Dory, take Queenie down the hall to show her the room," says Dory's mum, Maggie, who is a mum version of Dory.

We stand side by side in Dory's bedroom, looking at the mattress on his floor. A web of dread drapes across my internal organs.

"This is your room," I say. Obvious, much.

"Yep. And that's your bed." He points at the mattress. I gulp.

So I am going from never talking to a guy who is vaguely good-looking in my life to sharing a bedroom with him.

I drag my suitcase down the hall.

"Where are you going, Queenie?" calls Dory.

"Um, Mum, can I talk to you?" I hiss out the side of my mouth.

Mum is doing fancy hands as she talks to Maggie. She wraps an arm around my waist. "You can say it, Queenie!"

"In *private*," I say.

Mum raises her eyebrows at Maggie, as if to say, *I wonder what the big secret is.*

I drag Mum down the hall, still pulling my suitcase.

"Can't I share with you? Wouldn't that be more appropriate?" I say, trying to keep my voice low. I feel Maggie's and Dory's eyes on our backs.

"I'm just in a roll-out bed in the study, which Maggie says is very small," says Mum. "Also, Maggie thought it would be fun for you and Dory to have a slumber party! He doesn't know many people at the new school."

A slumber party?

"This is just for a night or two, yeah? Where are we going next?" I ask.

To my horror, Mum bites her lip.

"Well . . . I'm working on it," she says.

I give Mum a stare made of death.

I really wish now that I hadn't been so blasé about Pearl, the flaky house. I should have set up camp on Dimitri's front lawn and played his least favorite song over and over until he promised to prioritize our application.

"Queenie, I see what you are doing, and I am going to ask you right now to show a little gratitude," Mum says. Her tone is firmer than I am used to. There is no forced smile now. No gentle jokes. Mum means business. "The Elliots are kind enough to give us beds for a tiny amount of rent, which means I am not paying hundreds of dollars a night for an Airbnb we wouldn't get anyway."

"We could hit the road! Buy a camper van!" I plead. "I can pack light. We both can. Most of our stuff is in storage anyway."

Mum shakes her head and holds up two fingers. "Two words for you, Queenie Jean Anderson. Work. School. This conversation is over."

"But it's nearly summer break!" I cry.

"Nah-uh," says Mum, waggling her finger. "We're not living in a camper van. We have a perfectly good living situation right here. Until we find something more stable."

"Do you like chess, Queenie?" says Dory, approaching and taking my bag. "With a name like Queenie, I'd imagine you're a natural."

I silently follow Dory and my bag up the hall, wishing this, too, was easy to walk away from.

## seventeen

CHESS IS BORING. AND I'M BAD AT IT. Seven of my pieces, now captured, hug Dory's side of the board.

"You can't move the castle diagonally, remember?" says Dory gently.

I sigh.

"It's okay, Queenie. Move it back. We'll try again. Look where my queen is at. She's about to get you here and here. You need to move defensively if you've got any chance."

I study the board, my vision blurring. I reach for my knight just as Dory does. Our hands touch. I draw back and look away.

"Oops, sorry," mutters Dory. "You go."

I wait a second and try again. Dory smiles. "Yep! Excellent choice!"

"You play chess professionally, don't you?" I ask.

Dory chuckles. "Well, not professionally as such. Competitively, yes. I'm off to State this weekend, actually."

"They have State chess competitions?" I ask, my eyes wide. I try to imagine what that would be like. A crowd of people gathered around a chessboard. Two chess wizards wearing team colors. "Wow. State. That's pretty good."

Dory nods. "I've been in training since I could talk. And I love it! What do you love, Queenie?"

I try to think. I like a lot of things. Burgers at Miro's. Rom-coms.

"Guitar," I say. "And songwriting."

This second thing surprises me. Dory, though, looks impressed.

"Songwriting? Wow. I couldn't write a limerick to save myself. That's neat."

"Do you play an instrument?" I ask. I look around. There's no sign of an instrument.

"Nope. I'm not creative. I do tinker with Logic Pro. Do you know Logic?"

"That's what my favorite singer and her brother use to make her music," I say. "Billie Eilish. Her brother produces their songs in Logic Pro."

"Cool!" says Dory. I can see he's genuinely impressed.

I'm genuinely impressed.

My ability to make music goes as far as strumming notes on a guitar. But imagine the possibilities if you make music digitally.

"You sound pretty creative to me!" I say. Dory blushes.

"Hey, this is awkward to ask, but do you mind if I spend an hour training?" asks Dory. "I want to give this competition on Saturday everything I've got."

I nod and get up.

"Sorry about all this," I say, pointing to the chessboard. "I'm probably a lost cause."

"Everyone can learn," he says. "It just takes practice."

## eighteen

**I LIE ON MUM'S ROLL-OUT BED**, scrolling through old photos on her phone. I can hear her chatting with Maggie and Tim, Dory's dad, in the kitchen.

A message pops up on Mum's phone.

Dimitri.

It's just a smiley face. I'm tempted to click through and read the thread when Mum walks in.

"Dimitri messaged," I say, holding out the phone. "Is it about the house? Is he apologizing?"

"Mm," Mum says as she types. When she's done, she plonks on the roll-out bed next to me and downloads Facebook on her phone. Mum's not a big social media user, so I am curious to see what this is all about.

"Tim was just saying there's a Facebook group we can check out. Apparently, people post ads, looking for tenants. How about we have a look?"

I put my head on Mum's shoulder while she scrolls.

There's a room available in a shared house in downtown Curlew Point. But they only want a single female. No pets. No kids.

There are two rooms available in a cabin way out of town. But again, no kids.

Most of the posts, though, aren't houses looking for tenants. They are tenants looking for houses. Pictures of smiling faces grouped together in selfie poses. Their posts are full of heart emojis and smiley faces.

Hi! We are the Jamisons! We've been looking for five months for a home and are living in our camper van for now. We love organic food and are nonsmokers. We're looking for something peaceful ideally, within reach of the beaches and local schools. But will take anything. Most grateful for your help.

Hi. We have unexpectedly found ourselves without a home. I'm a single mum, with two kids, in kindergarten and third grade. Very respectful. Nonsmoker. No pets. Any assistance is appreciated.

Hi, folks,

My ten-year-old daughter and I are looking for a place to call our own. It's just us and our five-year-old schnauzer, Lucy. Kind, respectful, will do your gardening. We are ideally looking for a loving, conscious space.

The posts go on and on. Mum's eyes swim with tears.

"Are you okay, Mum?" I ask.

"Yep," she says. "I just didn't realize how bad it was. All these poor people without homes."

I curl in next to her. All these poor people and us.

"We should post something in the group," I say, pretending to take a selfie with Mum. I smile cheesily. "Mum and daughter. Super cool. Looking for a beautiful Queenslander home with lots of natural light. Close to beaches and shops."

Mum sighs. She's not smiling for the fake selfie. "I hate having to plead like that," she says. "Makes us sound so desperate."

Maybe we are. Desperate, that is.

# nineteen

WE SIT AROUND THE ELLIOTS' TINY DINING ROOM TABLE, eating dinner. When I think they're not looking, I look from Maggie to Tim to Dory. They're a sweet family, using their manners every chance they get. They're all *thank you* and *pass the salt, please.*

"Dory tells me you write music, Queenie," says Maggie.

I flinch, looking over at Dory.

"You do?" says Mum. "I didn't know that! Since when?"

"Daisy's been teaching the class songwriting," Dory explains. "Not my cup of tea. But Queenie's really good at it."

I blush so hard, I swear my cheeks are going to burn off. I look at my lasagna. Tim makes excellent lasagna.

"Oh, that's so great!" says Maggie. "You're going to enter the Wilsons Head Summer Song Contest, then?"

I look up. "I don't know about it," I say.

"It's on an outdoor stage near the beach. They were thinking of canceling it because of COVID safety stuff. But I hear through the council grapevine that they've just given it the okay to go ahead. Sixteenth of January."

"You should enter, Queenie!" says Dory, beaming at me. "Wilsons Head is only a couple of hours away!"

"Er." I take a tiny bite of lasagna. All the flavor has magically evaporated. My mouth has gone dry.

I can't get onstage to sing my favorite song in front of the school.

I can't get onstage to sing my favorite Christmas carol in front of my friends at the old people's village.

How on earth am I ever going to get onstage in front of strangers and sing one of my original songs? I so can't see this ever happening.

Maggie is doing something on her phone. She hands it to me.

"Here's the online form. Fill it in. The entries close this weekend. You don't want to miss out. Since I'm on the council, I can waive the entry fee for you. So no excuses!"

I feel them all watch me as I plug my details into Maggie's phone, song title TBA. I hand the phone back to Maggie.

Mum's grinning hard. She's also putting something in her phone. She holds it up to me.

"It's in the work calendar, see! Which means Sue can't double-book me. There's no way I am going to miss this!"

I prod my lasagna, not able to speak a word.

# twenty

**QUEENIE JEAN ANDERSON HAS FEW QUALITIES.** But one of them is the ability to sleep like a hibernating bear. I can sleep through a tornado, Mum tells me. Mum boasts that she trained me when I was a baby by watching YouTube on her phone next to my head while I slept.

Tonight, though, I'm restless. The thoughts of the Summer Song Contest are itching around my brain. Also, Dory's moving around in his bed, which is right beside mine. Even if I wanted to forget I was sharing a room with a kinda good-looking chess wizard, he's making it impossible.

I must have fallen asleep eventually, because all of a sudden, I am swimming through darkness in a swampy tunnel of light. My eyes slowly adjust to the lamplight as I try to work out where the heck I am and who the boy is on the bed next to me.

"What ya doing, Dory?" I ask, my words sticky with sleep.

Dory is sitting up in bed, his bedside lamp directed at the big board that rests against his knees. His tongue pokes out. He is drawing something in pencil.

I check my wristwatch.

2:03 a.m.

I kneel and peer over Dory's knees to see what he's doing. My gasp is involuntary.

Dory has drawn the most incredible portrait of me.

I know that sounds boastful. And I don't mean it in that way. My teeth protrude from too many years of thumb sucking and a strong aversion to braces. My nose is freckly. My hair is chaotic.

But jeez Louise. The kid can really draw.

"I never knew you could draw," I say. "You told me you weren't creative."

Dory doesn't seem to hear me. He's using an eraser to shade the contours of my cheeks.

"You never draw at school. Why? You're amazing."

"Huh" is all Dory says. Then eventually, "People would tease me."

"They wouldn't!" I say. "They would worship at your feet. You are very talented, Dory."

Dory is even better than the charcoal artist from the gallery. He could be famous! Forget chess.

He blows eraser debris away and holds the portrait out at arm's length. He nods and hands it to me. I study it. It really is a masterpiece.

"It's for you," says Dory. I'm still gawking at the portrait as Dory pulls on an eye mask, ducks under his covers, and reaches to switch off his light.

"'Night, Queenie," he says in the dark. "It's nice having you here."

I place the portrait beside me, next to Garfield, and gaze at it in the dark.

## twenty-one

"THE BUS LEAVES IN FIVE AND A HALF MINUTES, QUEENIE.
If we speed-walk, we will easily make it," says Dory the
next morning.

I speed-walk after Dory. His long legs whir down the
street. I'm puffing hard, trying to keep up.

Sparrow is already on the bus, and of course hers is
the first face I see pressed against the glass. She pulls
back, breathes, then draws something in her fog.

A crown.

A pawn.

A big heart in between.

OMG. I could die. I just hope Dory hasn't seen.

"Sorry you bombed out at the Christmas concert,
Queenie," says Sparrow. "That must have sucked."

I grimace.

"Hi, Lili," I say, ignoring Sparrow. I know this will make Sparrow mad. Lili half waves. She drops her hand quickly when Sparrow glares at her.

Sparrow looks sharply between me and Dory.

"So what's the deal with you two? Have you moved in with Dory or something? This isn't the bus stop for Diamonds."

"We're living together," says Dory calmly.

My cheeks fire up.

Sparrow's own expression goes from surprised to interrogating.

"What, like a boyfriend-and-girlfriend type thing?" she asks, narrowing her eyes.

"Type thing," says Dory, sliding in next to me.

OMG.

*o o o*

I can't get Dory out of my head all day. This is a bad, bad situation. I can't have a crush on my roommate. This is a disaster!

I've never had a proper crush before. I've crushed on singers, even dead ones, like John Lennon. But never a real person in my actual life.

I understand now why people write songs about crushes. They're all-consuming. I barely even taste the Snickers bar Maggie packed in my lunch box.

I'm relieved to see that Daisy is teaching music again today. Mr. Grey had a doctor's appointment, apparently. The more classes we have with Daisy, the more I like her. If real estate agents are made in factories, Daisies are made in clouds.

"All right, pair up!" says Daisy.

I'm about to ask Dory, but Sally is next to me, looking up at me expectantly.

"I'll be your partner, Queenie!" says Sally.

"Yeah, okay, Sally."

"Dory?" I hear Sparrow say. I look up sharply. *Don't do it, Dory. Don't do this to me.*

Dory doesn't have ESP, it turns out. He and Sparrow are a team. I know my face looks like death on a stick.

"Queenie? Are you okay? This is working, right?" asks Sally. She's transcribing our song into sheet music.

I try to focus. I try to not let Dory and Sparrow's conversation ruin my favorite class of the week.

We're working on giving our songs structure when Daisy takes a call on her cell phone. Being Daisy, and not a normal teacher, she sits on her desk and chats loudly, even though it's definitely not a work call. I can't help watching Daisy while Sally transcribes our song. She gazes out the window, her expression pinched.

"Terry's gone? No way! Man. That's tough, Ruthie . . . So you don't have another number for him? No . . . I don't, either. It's okay, Ruthie! Take a breath. We'll find someone! There are loads of people looking for homes right now!"

My stomach knots up. Terry's gone, which means Daisy needs a roommate. I know the situation at the Elliots' is just temporary. This thing at Daisy's could be something more permanent.

Also I don't know if I can feasibly exist sleeping next to my crush every night of the week till the end of time.

## twenty-two

"HOW DID YOUR AND SPARROW'S SONG GO?" I ask Dory that evening. We have a deal. Dory will not teach me chess. And I'll let him draw Garfield. I lie on Dory's bed next to him, studying his technique. I'm hoping that sharing a room with Dory will mean this amazing drawing ability will reach me by osmosis.

Dory doesn't answer. He's focusing on Garfield's creepy dimples.

"Is Sparrow a good songwriter?" I ask.

"Hm," says Dory. "She's okay. Her song is a bit clichéd. Like every other song you've ever heard. Are you ever going to play me one of yours?" He puts the drawing aside and sits up.

"Well . . . it's not really something I typically share with other people," I say.

"Aren't you lined up to play at the Summer Song Contest?" he says.

"Right. Yes. I suppose."

"Then test it out on me."

I hesitate. Then pick up my guitar. I start playing the tune I've been mucking around with. I come in with the words eventually. Quiet at first.

I stop.

"That's it. I've only written two verses."

Dory's grinning widely. "Now that's what I am talking about! That's original and, wow—Queenie. I love it. You're gifted."

I want to say thank you. But my voice is stuck.

Gifted? Dory really thinks so?

"I'm going to record you. Sit over here," says Dory, holding out his computer chair.

He sets up a program on his computer, puts his gaming mic on my head, and holds up his finger. "Okay, one second. All right. You can play."

I play my song. It's better now that I've already had a run-through.

Dory mucks around with the program as I sit there holding Dad's guitar. I watch his long fingers stroke the keyboard and move the mouse around. The green shapes on the screen lengthen and shorten.

He saves the file: *Queenie.*

I don't know why, but this feels really special.

"Hey, you can help me with my song," he says, sitting back on the bed. "Mine's terrible."

"Give me a word," I say.

"Huh?" Dory looks perplexed.

"Any word! Whatever springs to mind."

"Um . . ." He gazes around the room. He settles on Garfield. "Gnome."

"Great!" I say. "Give me another word."

Looking encouraged, Dory calls out, "Computer!"

"Great!"

"Sock!"

"Love it."

"Chess!"

I scribble down Dory's words thick and fast. A stream of everything Dory can see and experience in the immediate present.

"Queen!" he says. He looks straight at me when he says it, his irises quavering. A tingle runs up my spine. "Aren't you going to write it down?" he asks.

"Yep. Queen," I say, scribbling. "Okay. Now we're going to put the words together in a song."

Dory checks his watch. "Oh, no. I have a meeting with my chess coach in five. Can I take a rain check?"

"You have a chess coach?" I say.

Dory grins. "Of course. I'm planning to be national champion."

o o o

Mum and I walk down Sentimental Avenue to get take-away Thai when she gets back from work. The evening is a balmy cloak.

"You and Dory seem to be getting on," says Mum. I see her biting back a grin.

"Yep, Dory is cool," I say. Mum raises her eyebrows. "By the way, I know a place we can move to! It could be awesome."

"Oh, yeah?"

I tell Mum about overhearing Daisy's conversation on the phone.

"You shouldn't eavesdrop" is all Mum can say.

"You don't understand! Daisy is awesome! She's not a real teacher. She's a sub. She has tattoos." Mum's frown deepens. I realize I have taken the wrong approach. Why would Mum want to move in with a person with tattoos who wasn't a real teacher? "I bet Daisy lives somewhere really nice. She has good fashion sense."

My words are swallowed up by the call of cicadas and cockatoos.

Mum hooks her arm into mine. "Queenie Pants, listen. We'll find a place. We just have to be patient. As Sarah says, the universe provides. Let's just focus on being in the moment, huh?"

My mind is ticking. I will ask Daisy directly. Get more information. That would be the sensible, grown-up thing to do.

o o o

We're inching toward the end of the term. Only two more days to go. Then we'll have a six-week break. You can sense the teachers are done with the term.

I have to run to catch Daisy before she disappears into the staff room.

"Daisy? Can. I. Ask. Something?" I say between pants. My side is stitched up.

Daisy beams and sweeps her curls out of her eyes. "Sure, Queenie! You know you and Sal are doing great with your song, don't you? You have the knack, lady. You should check out the Summer Song Contest over the break."

I grin. *Lady?*

"It's not about the song," I say. "It's—" I inspect my nails, wondering how to tell a teacher I've been listening to her personal conversations and want to move in with her. I remember a podcast Mum and I listened to on our last trip to the city. It was about strength in vulnerability, and how being real—being yourself—is a pathway to connection.

If anyone will respect real, it's Daisy.

"Mum and I are kinda homeless," I say.

"Oh?" Daisy's expression changes. She cocks her head so that her hair falls in a long wave. "That sucks," she says.

"We are living with Dory's family for now. But it would be amazing to actually live somewhere, you know, like in a place of our own."

"So many people are struggling to find homes right now," says Daisy. "It's a totally weird time. Did you know even Mrs. Doherty can't find a place to live?" Mrs. Doherty is the principal. She wears a three-piece suit and does *not* look like the sort of woman who should be left out on the street. "My sister and her boyfriend are living in a bus! I told them to pull up on our property, until they sort themselves out. Our landlord would be cool with it, I figure."

*What about Terry?* I want to say.

Daisy tips her head in the other direction. "You know, if you and your mum get really stuck, there's a place on the property where I live. Our friend Terry just moved out. It needs renovating, but, you know. It could work for a while."

I am hugging Daisy before I even know what I am doing. It takes me a moment to realize this is totally inappropriate. I jump back and knock straight into Mrs. James, the fourth-grade teacher, who purses her lips in displeasure and strides off.

Daisy grins. "I'll email your mum tonight," she says.

## twenty-three

**I SPEND THE AFTERNOON HANGING OUT** with Audrey and Walter at Diamonds. Audrey is getting a Christmas-themed pedicure when I arrive. Walter is back in his undies, sitting beside her.

"Queenie!" she says. "How's it all going? Are you moving back anytime soon?"

"Unlikely," I say. "We might be moving in with this cool teacher, Daisy. She's a musician, too."

"Sounds great," says Audrey, wriggling her toes. I catch Walter looking over at her adoringly. OMG. Cuteness overload.

I fill Audrey and Walter in on everything that's happened since leaving Diamonds. Audrey seems to be particularly fixated on Dory.

"Well, is he very good-looking? On a scale of ten, if one is hideous and ten is Arnold Schwarzenegger."

I grin. "Eight. He's no Arnie. He's his own kind of good-looking."

"I say go for it," says Walter, which is really unhelpful.

o o o

"Queenie, did you ask your teacher if we can move in with her?" Mum finds me in Dory's room that evening. Dory's off at chess practice. I am tacking the portrait he made me to the bit of wall under the window. Dory said it can be a wall of my very own. He even gave me a strip of his Blu-Tack.

"Daisy offered," I say without turning around. I feel Mum's eyes bore into me.

"She did, did she? Likely story. Well, the place is miles out of town. And I don't know if you realize this, but it's a camper van rather than a house. Apparently, it has a leak. I'm going to politely turn Daisy's offer down."

I hear Mum's sneakers disappear down the hall.

A camper van?

Anyway, it doesn't matter. Mum will be emailing Daisy right this moment—thank you, but no thank you very much.

o o o

That night, Dory and I lie on our beds. Even though
Maggie has already called lights-out, the lamp is on and
we're both drawing against our knees. I am trying out
Dory's shading technique. Dory hums.

"What's the tune?" I ask. "It's nice."

"Don't know," says Dory.

"Did you make it up? I don't think I've ever heard it
before."

Dory doesn't reply. He does hum louder, though. I take
this as my cue. I pick up Dad's guitar and try to match the
chords to Dory's tune. It takes a few goes. But eventually
my playing and Dory's humming meet in the middle.

"Chessboard, ah, ah. Sock and gnome. Your computer
queen!" I sing along.

Dory chuckles. He joins in. We keep adding random
words. The words stretch outside the perimeter of the
room. We're singing about lasagna and Sparrow Hawkins
and dandelions in the park. Dory holds my gaze the whole
time. I move up to the bed so I can get a better position
with the guitar. When I do, Dory leans in toward me.

I freeze. I think I am playing. I'm not sure.

He puts his hand on mine. Leans closer. Our noses
touch. Then our teeth.

His lips are on mine. I'm hanging there in midair, kissing Dory Elliot.

Time bends.

The spell is broken by Maggie's high-pitched voice from the door.

"What on earth!" We pull apart. I slide off the bed and bury my head, mortification filling me like concrete. I can hear Maggie's silence looming for eons. Then, "Under our roof, Queenie? Really? When we were so kind to let you and your mother . . ." Maggie's words are scratchy. I feel ill. Maggie is right. I've ruined everything. Mum will never forgive me.

I sneak a glance up at Dory, who is smiling. He gazes down at me.

A million feelings race through me. I can't make out what they are called, or if they are right, wrong, or upside down. Maggie cuts through the traffic.

"Queenie, you can sleep in your mum's room tonight," she says, her voice slim and hard.

I gather my camping mattress, quilt, and pillow and slide past her, trying not to make contact with her, with Dory, with the world. Ideally, I could disappear permanently right now.

I don't tell Mum what happened. I know that Maggie will fill her in first thing in the morning. Instead, I curl under my quilt, my head buried, trying to remember the way Dory's kiss felt.

I know what Billie Eilish says about kisses. But until this evening, I hadn't thought *properly* about them. I hadn't thought I would actually ever kiss someone. Kissing was something other people did. Songwriters. Grown-ups. Audrey and Walter. Anyone but me.

No matter how many times I smack my lips, the tingle doesn't go away. I find myself wishing Dory were next to me rather than Mum so I could reach across and try it all again.

*the third move*
# CAMPER VAN

## twenty-four

**IT'S POURING RAIN THE DAY WE MOVE** into Daisy's land-lord's camper van. The rain comes down in iron sheets, so loud and hard that Mum has to crawl while driving around the tight corners, her body pressed to the steering wheel so she can see.

We haven't spoken since we left the Elliots'.

I know she'll thaw. Mum's a chatterer, and I am the main person she's got to talk to. When she lets herself see the funny side of this whole mess, things will go back to normal. Great, even! Just me and Mum in a camper van. We'll have bonfires with my favorite teacher, and I'll write songs under the stars. Maybe we'll get chickens.

Dory won't be there. But . . . chickens.

The road seems to wind on for hours. We're deep in the hills. Suddenly, water gushes on either side of us. The car swerves. Mum revs. Her little car makes it out of the water.

Just.

"Bloody hell," says Mum. I'm not used to hearing her swear. "I shouldn't have driven through that causeway. People get swept away doing that."

Soon after the creek, we turn onto a dirt track. The rain has made deep ridges on either side of the road, so Mum's little car teeters precariously in the middle. At some point, we sink and emerge from a massive pothole, which makes my stomach lurch.

"You have arrived at your destination," says the GPS lady.

Mum stops the car. We're not anywhere. We can hardly see, either. Mum opens her car door, and rain soaks her seat. I sit there for a bit, but realize that if anyone is going to greet Daisy, it should be me. I pull my hoodie over my head and duck out of the car.

Mum and I dash down the steep driveway. When Mum nearly trips, I grab her elbow to steady her. She pulls away and runs ahead.

Lights glow in the main house. Even though it's summer, a plume of smoke dances out of the chimney.

If it gets the slightest bit cool, north coasters will light a fire, guaranteed. It's a subtropical symptom.

We both pummel the door, desperate to get inside, out of the wet.

"Hi! Daisy said—" starts Mum when a round lady in denim overalls over a bra opens the door. The woman pulls us inside and slams the door behind us.

"Heya! I'm Ruthie!" She hugs Mum.

"Oh!" says Mum into Ruthie's armpit.

Ruthie grabs me, hugs me, then holds me at arm's length. She smells like earth.

"You're Queenie," she says. I nod.

"This is my place," says Ruthie, still holding one of my shoulders. "Daisy's in the shed out the back with her girlfriend, Sonny. Xen lives in the garage with her little girl, Tara. And you two are gonna have the camper van! We're back to being a land of ladies, now that Terry's done a runner. Do you feel like broth?"

She doesn't wait for an answer. She's already ladling brown liquid into chipped bowls.

"It's a bit of a rat's nest, sorry," says Ruthie. "Been delivering babies all weekend and haven't had a chance to get on top of things. Now, all the rain. Sheesh. I was lucky to make it across the causeway just in time. You got a four-wheel drive, I hope. You got over the causeway okay?"

Mum nods. "Just," she says. "Is it like that every time it rains? I don't have a four-wheel drive. I drive a bucket."

Ruthie chortles. "Well, you could be in trouble, then! Yep, that causeway goes under after a day of heavy rain. Lucky we live in paradise, hey! No better place to be stuck for a week."

Ruthie plonks the bowls in front of us. Broth splashes onto the table. I dip in a spoon and flinch when the soup burns my tongue. I feel Mum's dismay radiate. Mum's never missed a day of work in her life. She's scratching the bad spot on her arm.

"Is Daisy here?" I ask.

"She and Sonny are tucked away in their shed. We'll see them in a bit for dinner. We eat together every night out here. Some communities don't dig communal living. But when it works, it works. I, for one, like the company."

Ruthie eases into one of the mismatched chairs at the table. It creaks with her weight. I gaze around her house. Everything seems broken and chipped. A sheet hangs over the couch. Another hangs from the stair banister. Feathers hang from a dream catcher in the middle of the room. There's a layer of dust on every surface. Plates and pots clutter the kitchen counter. There's a giant bone lying on a plate beside the soup pot.

"You're a midwife, Ruthie?" asks Mum.

"Yep! Twenty-five years and counting. That's nearly three thousand babies! Not bad, huh. There's nothing more special than bringing a newborn into this world. Never gets old."

"Mum works at Diamonds. The other end of the system," I say, blowing on my soup. "She escorts people out of the world."

"Queenie," scolds Mum. But Ruthie is grinning.

"Ha! Yep. The caring profession is an honorable one. Whether you are looking after babies or nursing people on the tail end, you are doing something good with your life. That's what I believe. Making an actual difference."

Daisy and her girlfriend come in soon after, holding hands. Daisy's barefoot. Her girlfriend, Sonny, has a side cut and a nose ring like Daisy's.

Daisy wraps me in a shoulder cuddle. She smells like sandalwood. It feels different from when I hugged her at school. This cuddle belongs perfectly in Ruthie's wooden kitchen. Sonny, too, hugs me. She pecks both my cheeks. Then kisses Mum.

"Welcome to Shoestring Creek!" says Sonny, her accent vaguely foreign. French, maybe?

"Queenie's the most amazing songwriter!" Daisy tells Sonny as they take a seat at the round table.

I shrug. "Daisy's been teaching us," I say. "At school."

Mum's eyes stay on me.

"Have you met Xen yet?" asks Daisy, her expression dancing.

"Oh, stop that, Daisy," chides Ruthie.

"Stop what? I didn't say anything."

"Giving Xen a hard time. You know you are." Ruthie tuts and shakes her head.

"I wasn't! I love Xen!" says Daisy. Then to Mum and me, "Xen is a self-professed healer. Spends some time with the angels. But mostly, she's a darling. Just don't let her read your palms."

The rain marches on, vibrating the tin roof of Ruthie's house. Just then, the door swings open. A little kid with no top on and knotty hair tears in and jumps into Ruthie's lap. She closes her eyes, resting against Ruthie. Ruthie kisses the kid's hair.

"This, as you've probably guessed, is Tara. Named after the Hindu Great Goddess. Mother Creator. Guess what? I was the first person to meet Tara ever. Even before her mum!"

"Ruthie birfed me," says Tara, looking around the table proudly. Some of her teeth are missing. The few that are left are small and brown. One is chipped badly.

"Yours was a magical birth, wasn't it, Tara?" says Ruthie. "Your totem python slid into the cabin to keep watch over you. It was a full moon. A clear sky. Your mother was a goddess, too."

I wriggle uncomfortably, imagining a python sliding into the cabin. I inspect the door, then the floor under my feet. When I'd enthusiastically put my hand up for the spare camper van at Daisy's place, I hadn't thought about pythons.

"Where's Xen, Tara?" asks Ruthie. "Is she joining us for dinner?"

"Levitating," says Tara. I assume that Tara has misused the word. Levitating is when you lift off the ground. People don't really lift off the ground. That sort of thing only happens in movies and mythology.

Daisy smiles at Tara.

After dinner, Mum and I wash up. When there's a break in the rain, Daisy and Sonny walk with us to the top of the driveway to collect our suitcases because Mum's still too scared to drive down the rippled driveway in her sardine can. Tara runs shirtless beside us, jumping barefoot into puddles. I sidestep so I don't get sprayed in red mud. We see a rainbow bending over the ridge. Three black cockatoos swirl overhead, calling.

"They are telling us there's going to be more rain," Tara says.

"Great," says Mum.

Mum jostles the door of Terry's camper. It takes a few goes, but it eventually comes unstuck. True to description, the camper is leaky. A stream of water trickles down one wall. A line of mold decorates one of the other walls. The kitchen counter is saggy with moisture. There's an epic stain of some terrible nature in the center of the only bed. I shudder imagining what made the stain. The place smells of mold and rotting leaf litter. I want to throw open every window so I can breathe. But the rain has started again.

Mum just raises her eyebrows at me, unzips her suitcase, and unpacks in silence.

## twenty-five

**MUM HAS TO LEAVE FOR HER SHIFT AT DIAMONDS** before it's even light the next morning so she can make it on time. It's the last day of school. I plead with Mum to let me stay home and help Ruthie plant seedlings in the veggie patch. But Mum has already asked Daisy if I can ride into school with her. She's subbing for Mrs. McMillan from kindergarten today because Mrs. McMillan started break a week early.

We bump around in Daisy's ancient pickup truck. The rain is a soft mist. Daisy keeps the windows down, her elbow hooked on the window ledge and one hand on the steering wheel.

"Any new songs?" asks Daisy.

"Not really," I say. I don't tell her about the song I've written in my head about my first kiss. She might ask me where my inspiration comes from. I might accidentally blush. I might accidentally tell her about Dory Elliot.

No.

Way.

Daisy hums to herself. She doesn't seem to mind not talking. I watch her long tanned limbs move with every bump and the tattoo of the dragon shimmer in the mist.

"Why did you choose a dragon?" I ask.

Daisy laughs. "Dragons are fierce. I like fierce," she says.

"You're not very fierce yourself," I say. "You're pretty much the nicest teacher at Curlew Point."

"Ha! That's because I'm not really a teacher," says Daisy.

"You're not? But I thought you were a substitute."

"Yeah, I'm a sub. For now. I have a teaching qualification. But teaching's not my dream."

"What is? Music?"

Daisy shrugs. "'Course I love making music. But, nah. My dream's just a silly dream. Not very realistic."

Now I am curious. I can't help asking.

"You can tell me. I won't think it's silly. Promise."

Daisy bites her bottom lip. She looks over at me again.

"Okay, don't judge me, but I actually want to be a doctor."

This surprises me. I don't know why. Maybe because I have never seen a doctor with a nose ring and a tattoo.

"Why don't you become a doctor, then?" I ask.

"Ten years at medical school. Plus, I might not get in. You have to pass this fierce exam called the GAMSAT. I'd have to go over all my twelfth-grade chemistry, biology, and physics again, and study really hard, just to have a shot at passing."

"Why do you want to be a doctor?" I ask.

Daisy thinks for a while before she answers. "To help people in developing countries," she says. "We don't feel the effects of the pandemic so much here in Australia. But kids around the world are suffering right now. Really suffering. It'd be cool to actually make a difference. Not just talk about it."

Daisy does make a difference, just being Daisy. If it hadn't been for Daisy, I wouldn't have discovered songwriting. Or have a place to live.

But my problems are champagne problems, as Mum would say.

Suddenly, I really want Daisy to be a doctor. I've never wanted anything more in my life.

"I could help you study. For your test," I say before thinking it out. I have no idea what the difference is between chemistry, biology, and physics, as my school lumps them together and calls it "physical science." But the offer is out there now, floating around the truck.

Daisy smiles. "Queenie, you're the best. You know what? That would be awesome. Sonny is so not interested in studying."

I can't wipe the smile off my face when I step down from Daisy's truck in the staff parking area. Adelaide James, Mrs. James's daughter, who is in my grade, is getting out of her mum's car next to us.

"Oh!" says Adelaide, looking between me and Daisy. "I didn't know you were related to a teacher."

"I'm not. Daisy and I are living together." I feel so übercool and grown-up. I am living with a teacher! Like, in a shared house. Kind of. And not just any teacher, either. A songwriting teacher with a dragon tattoo who wants to study medicine and help children in developing countries.

Daisy waves me off once we are through the school gates. "Enjoy your last day of school!" she calls.

I stride across the quadrangle. I feel like some of Daisy's tattoo rubbed off on me, and no one can mess with me. Not even Sparrow Hawkins.

Sparrow pulls out of the four-square game especially to walk beside me.

"How's Dory? Mmm, mmm, mmwa!" She makes kissing noises into her hand.

"Not sure," I say. "We're living with Daisy now."

I sneak a glance. Sure enough, Sparrow's expression is spiked with jealousy. Just a hint, but enough to make me feel 100 percent amazing.

"What, Daisy Daisy?" Sparrow says.

"Daisy schoolteacher Daisy." I know I am smirking. I know smirking doesn't suit me, or suit anyone. But I can't help it.

"That's so weird, living with a teacher" is all Sparrow can say before trailing away from me.

Sparrow is easy to manage, I realize. I have years of experience being a tortoise. My shell is rock hard, and she drips off me like swamp water.

Dory, on the other hand . . .

I feel like I am holding my breath all day, looking for Dory. He's not in homeroom when Mrs. James does roll call. He's not in math class. He's nowhere on the playground. He must be away.

He could be training.

He could be sick.

Or he could be avoiding me. The thought makes me feel sick. One happy sick circle.

It shouldn't matter. It's summer vacation as of

tomorrow. I wouldn't have seen Dory for another six weeks anyway. But I was kind of hoping we could exchange email addresses.

Now it's going to be like the kiss never happened.

"Queenie?" Mr. Grey is striding toward me.

"Hi, Mr. Grey." He stands awkwardly, as if he's not sure what to do with his hands.

"So—last day of school, huh?"

"Yep," I say. "Sorry about the end-of-year concert. And the posters and all that."

Mr. Grey shrugs. "Look, Queenie. I get it. You're not a performer. And I've realized that you don't have to be. But you have to promise me you'll never stop playing guitar, okay?" He squeezes my shoulder. Ouch.

I nod, mainly to get him to stop squeezing my shoulder. "I promise I won't stop playing guitar," I say. "And thanks for, erm, being my music teacher."

Mr. Grey heats up to the top of his bald head. "Well, it's my job. Good luck out there, Queenie."

He strides off—long legs in silky trousers.

Inspiration on a stick.

At the end of the day, I clear out my locker. Right at the back, there's something scrolled up tight. I unroll it and grin.

A pencil drawing of Garfield grins back at me.

## twenty-six

**EVERY KID IN THE SCHOOL MAKES A TUNNEL** with their hands for us sixth graders as we leave the school gates for the very last time. I am practically on my knees trying to crawl under the cute kindergarten kids' arms. They touch each other's fingertips and grin at us.

"Bye!"

"Bye!"

"Good luck!" they chant.

Daisy's waiting out front, her back against the gate and one Doc Marten resting against her calf.

"Queenie! Your mum texted," says Daisy. "She says something's come up and she'll be late getting home. She asked me to give you a lift. Is that cool?"

"Totally cool," I say. "Did Mum say what came up?"
Mum always meets me at the bus stop or the school gates.
It's one of the perks of having worked at Diamonds for so
long. They let her off early to come meet me. Missing the
last school pickup ever is a bit weird.

"Nah," says Daisy. "Just says she'll be home after dinner."

When we're back at Shoestring Creek, Daisy lets me
hang out with her in her room. I sit on her bed with my
guitar. Daisy's nursing her ukulele. Other than playing to
Dory two nights ago, I don't usually play in front of other
people. But Daisy swears Billie is also her favorite musician, and I can't resist jamming with her.

"How are you feeling about school being over?" asks
Daisy between tunes.

"It's fine," I say. "Just feels like another day."

Graduation is this big black unknown in my periph-
eral vision. I know it's there. I know it's probably scary.
But it's out of touch and out of reach.

Right now, all I want is Daisy and our music. I can't
think about upper school.

The only other person on the property right now is
Tara. She is on the floor, beading a necklace out of dried
seedpods.

"How was school today?" I ask Tara when Daisy has had
enough of ukulele and starts painting her nails turquoise.

"I don't go to school," she says. "School restricts the imagination."

I hold back my smile. Tara sounds like she's seventy, not seven. This must be something her mum says. Speaking of which, I still haven't met Xen. I am starting to think she might not exist. Could Tara be a wild forest child, born of the trees and the eagles? It feels like she could be.

"Does your mum teach you at home?" I ask.

"No," says Tara.

"Xen believes in unlearning," says Daisy. She swipes a layer of polish on her big toenail. "It's where you let the child follow their interests and passions. You don't actually teach kids, as such."

I've never heard of unlearning. But it sounds kind of fun. If I'd been unlearned, I would have studied guitar riffs on YouTube. I could have been a concert guitarist by now—a real Andrés Segovia—if school hadn't been holding me back.

But I wouldn't have met Daisy.

I fall into a new made-up rhythm and sing my song softly under my breath. Daisy looks up, smiling. She hums a harmony.

Tara grins between us.

"That sounds very pretty," she says. "Keep singing!"

○ ○ ○

I eat tofu and stir-fried vegetables with Daisy, Sonny, and Tara. Ruthie is at a home birth. And Mum's still not back.

"How's Audrey?" I ask Mum when she finally returns.

We squelch through the mud toward our camper. It's already pitch-black so we light our way using Mum's phone. The cicadas are screaming.

"Audrey? She had a good morning, I think," she says. "Her usual self."

"Didn't you just come from Diamonds?" I narrow my eyes at Mum even though she can't see me in the dark.

"Oh. Yep." Mum slips out of her boots before opening the camper door. I cough as the mold races into my lungs. "I see what you mean. Audrey's fine. Asking after you as always. Now that it's summer vacation, you have six weeks to spend with her!"

I'm grateful Mum's thawed toward me. Sleeping in one manky bed together does that. But she's quiet tonight, which is still very un-Mum. She looks weird, too. Not bad weird. Good weird. Like she's holding in a secret. She keeps glancing at her phone, like it's in on the secret.

"Did you find a place for us?" I ask. "Something bigger and less moldy? I don't even care if it's not a Queenslander. Or even if it's not pretty."

"So very flexible," she says, smiling.

"Well, did you?" I ask.

"No," says Mum. "But something will come. When the stars align. Anyway, the market is changing after summer. Dimitri says people will head back to the city. Guaranteed. And there'll be more homes again for locals."

"Dimitri?"

Mum shrugs. "Well, he's a real estate agent. I guess it's his job to know things like that."

Even though I am boring into Mum with my interrogating stare, she goes about the camper, humming, brushing her teeth, and moisturizing.

I notice her skin is looking better. Maybe camper life isn't so bad for us after all.

*o o o*

The rain starts again in the middle of the night, hammering our little camper senseless. I pull my pillow over my head. Mum groans.

We're so close, in the small bed. Sleeping next to Mum is like sleeping next to a heater. Mum and I used to share a bed when I was little, and again when Dad died. I don't think I had my own bed until I was six or seven, when Mum got sick of me hogging the blanket.

"I can't sleep," I say after a while.

"Neither," says Mum.

It's just after three a.m. We sit up against the camper wall, our blanket over our knees, Mum's phone glowing in the dark. We're watching the final season of *Gilmore Girls*, which has become our all-time favorite show. Mum used to watch it before I was born, and she's watching it again with me. A mum and daughter who hang out like friends. Just like Mum and me.

The episode keeps glitching, on account of bad reception. Also, we can barely hear it, the rain's so loud.

My back feels wet against the wall. I squirm to change position. But my bum is soaked, too.

"Oh, jeez!" says Mum, leaping up. "Water's coming through the roof!"

We slap the wall, our bed, and the roof with tea towels, blankets, dirty laundry. But they all soak through.

"We can't sleep like this!" I say. Our hair is plastered down with wet. Our pajamas soaked. It doesn't matter for me. I'm on summer break. But Mum's supposed to be at work in a few hours.

"I probably can't cross the causeway to get to work," says Mum. She stands on the wet bed and presses her pillow against the ceiling. Droplets run down her nose, into the mattress. "Text Sue from my phone, Queenie."

I go to text Sue. I can't help noticing that Dimitri's the last person who texted Mum.

See you soon, beautiful.

I swallow. This relationship no longer seems very professional.

I text Sue about Mum not getting into work because of the natural disaster and go back to soaking our stuff with rain.

We last another ten minutes. Mum's arms are quavering. Everything's wet.

"Let's go to the main house!" Mum calls over the rain.

"What about our stuff?" I yell.

"Forget it!"

I pat under the bed for Dory's Garfield and the portrait he made of me. They're flimsy tissue paper. They disintegrate in my hands. I feel like sobbing.

"Dad's guitar!" I say.

"Come on, Queenie! It looks like the roof is going to cave in!"

I grab the guitar and wrap it in my hoodie.

We leap out of the camper, ankle-deep into a muddy puddle. I'm barefoot and soaked through, so what's a puddle?

Mum's trying to use her phone as a light under her top. But the rain is too much. We run through the dark, through the pouring rain.

"Argh!" I cry as I step on something soft.

The soft thing leaps away. A cane toad! I shudder. They're the worst. More cane toads leap across our pathway. The path to Ruthie's goes on and on forever.

We bang on the door. There are no lights on because it's three a.m. Mum goes over to the window. She taps and presses her face against the glass.

"I don't see her!" Mum calls.

"She's probably still at the birth," I call back.

We open Ruthie's door, hoping she won't mind, and spill, dripping wet, into the kitchen.

Mum turns on the kitchen light and manages to get the fire going so we can dry out a bit. I put on the kettle to make us tea. We huddle in front of the fire, under blankets, staring out at the rain plastering the window.

"Paradise, hey," mutters Mum.

*the fourth move*
# RUTHIE'S HOUSE

## twenty-seven

**THE RAIN KEEPS COMING FOR DAYS.** Ruthie's stuck on the other side of the causeway, still staying with the new mum and baby. Sonny is also stuck in town. It's just us, Daisy, Xen, and Tara. Xen's been in her room meditating most of the time, so we haven't seen much of her. When I do see her, she barely talks. It's like she's hardly there at all. I see what Daisy meant about her being with the angels. I almost want to pinch her to check if she's real.

After three days of rain, the wind finally eases. It feels like there's a gap in the weather, even though it's still raining. I pull on Ruthie's oilskin jacket and plug myself into her rain boots. I trudge through the sheets of rain to check the causeway.

A brown ocean spills over the thin road. I'm so glad Mum made it back before the creek rose.

"What ya doing?" asks Tara.

She's a thin little thing, in her underwear, which is drenched. She's still barefoot and caked in mud. I pull her under the oilskin to try to keep her a bit dry.

The rain is harder now, and the wind picks up again.

"Let's check out the camper," I say, pulling her under my jacket.

Cane toads cover the garden, loving the wet. There's a huge branch on the camper roof, which must have come down in the storm.

I try to pull the camper door open. But it's stuck. I press my face to the glass. It's dark inside. I can't see a thing.

"It's ruined," says Tara, pressing against me.

"Maybe," I say.

When we're almost back at the main house, I turn back. The camper's roof has definitely caved in.

I decide not to say anything to Mum. I don't want to worry her. I don't want her to start thinking of options for a new home. We've only just gotten here.

*o o o*

It's been raining solidly now for five days. The power has cut off a few times, so we've had to light Ruthie's emergency candles. Mum's worried about missing so much work, and when the power's working, she calls in to give updates. She tells me Sue's found someone to cover her shifts for now. But I know how much Mum hates letting them down.

Tara, Daisy, Mum, and I while away the days playing board games, charades, music. Even Xen's been out more the last few days. The music sessions are my favorite. Xen plays the Caribbean steel drum, which is a beautiful instrument. Tara tinkles on the tambourine. Mum doesn't play an instrument, so she just sings.

We go through every song I've ever learned. Songs by the Rolling Stones. The Beatles. Led Zeppelin. Billie Eilish. Dolly Parton. Tom Waits. "Silent Night."

Daisy teaches me new songs, which is cool. I've never had a guitar teacher. Only YouTube. It's amazing having someone to actually fix my finger work and help me find the harder notes.

"Play your original song, Queenie," says Daisy after one particularly long session. "It's sounding really good."

"Nah," I say.

"Come on, Queenie!" says Mum. "Please? I'm dying to hear it!"

I look at Daisy, who's beaming at me. I feel her confidence drip through me. She really believes in me. I would feel bad letting her down.

I shrug and start playing. Daisy joins in. Then Xen. The tingle whips through me. Electricity. My song, branching out through Ruthie's warm, people-filled house.

I sing the words. I have the whole song now.

*Take me back home,*

*Faded and gray.*

*We all move away,*

*One long summer's day.*

I open my eyes just in time to see Mum wipe tears away. I close my eyes again.

*The rain comes down violent,*

*Blood streaked, and silent.*

*Steam rises up.*

*We're stuck in a lane*

*Where we all feel the pain.*

The tune changes key here for the bridge.

*Race fast, chase fast,*

*Let's go.*

*Take heed, then go slow.*

*Even when you know it won't last—*

*Let's go.*

I slow the guitar. Daisy slows. Xen slows. My voice drops for the final verse.

*And then, when it's over, we lay in the field,*
*Our backs on the earth,*
*And stars in our eyes.*
*From faded and gray,*
*We've come here to stay,*
*We all fall away,*
*On that long summer's day.*

Daisy harmonizes on the last few lines. I swear I am melting. When I open my eyes, Mum launches at me. She buries me in a hug and sobs into my hair.

"Queenie Pants, it's bloody brilliant. Where did you come from? I swear . . ." she blubbers. "Your dad. Gosh, he would have loved to have heard this."

A smile plays on the edges of my mouth.

I don't think much about Dad. I hardly knew him, because I was only five when he passed away. But occasionally I fantasize about a world where Dad and I play music together—the sun setting behind us.

"It's lovely," says Xen dreamily. "I like writing poems, too."

She's whispering. It takes me a moment to realize she's reciting a poem about Gaia, the Earth Mother. I like

143

it, but it's hard to follow. I guess that's the thing about poetry and songwriting. Logic doesn't have to come into it. It's as much about feeling as meaning.

"You're going to win the Summer Song Contest, Queenie. You're going to be famous," says Daisy as we wash up.

"I don't really want to be famous," I say.

"What? Doesn't every twelve-year-old want to be famous?" she says.

"Not me. I just want to make music."

And I also want to get up in front of people and perform so I can feel what I just felt this afternoon in Ruthie's living room. That would also be nice.

But I am 100 percent sure I won't be doing the Summer Song Contest. I don't have it in me.

"I can understand that," says Daisy.

I catch myself gazing at Daisy. Even though we are technically flooded in and I have no way of contacting Dory, I'm lucky to be stuck here with Daisy.

Sparrow would hate this, but I am pretty sure Daisy and I are becoming good friends.

o o o

We're playing UNO that afternoon when things go quiet.

"The rain's stopped!" yells Tara.

She's out the front door in her underwear before anyone can stop her. When I make it out the door, I see Tara in the chicken coop, ankle-deep in mud, cuddling a soggy bantam.

A ray of sun strokes my face. I smile, soaking it in completely.

"I'm going out to check the camper and retrieve some stuff," says Mum, passing me in rain boots.

I trot after her as gigantic cane toads leap out of the way. Ugh.

It's not a good sign that water is trickling out from under the front door. Mum uses her whole body to yank the door free. Water gushes out, filling Mum's boots and soaking the bottom half of her jeans.

"Jeez Louise," I say, looking past Mum into the camper.

There's about half a meter of water filling the camper van as if it were a bathtub. Papers and clothes float through the brown water. A package of cookies. A rotting apple. Our suitcases are covered over. I am so glad I saved Dad's guitar. I wish I could say the same about Dory's portraits. They're the only other thing I actually care about, I realize.

Unlike the portraits, Garfield remains intact. He stands on the counter grinning proudly. A mascot of survival. I have to stretch to reach him over the water.

"Well done, Garfield," I say, patting his hat.

Garfield might be fine. But our home isn't. Our home is officially destroyed. Unlivable.

I get that good old sinking feeling in my belly. This means we're going to have to move again. Even though it's inconvenient to get flooded in, in another way I have kind of loved the last few days. The warmth of Ruthie's house. Daisy's and Xen's delicious soupy stews. The warm fire. Our music. My friendship with Daisy.

Mum sighs and steps away from the camper. She arches back, her hands on her hips, and stares up at the sky. "Really?" she yells. "COVID. Homelessness. Now flipping floods?"

I stare at Mum, bewildered. I've never seen her like this. She's chirpy Mum. Happy Mum. I'm usually the gloomy one.

I can't handle it.

She stomps the ground. It swallows her boot. She growls from her gut. Then roars. "Gah!"

Holy hell. This is serious.

Mum waves her phone around, trying to find good reception.

"Flipping reception!" she yells, trudging up the hill to the top of the driveway.

"Who are you calling?" I ask, chasing after her.

"I'm calling Dimitri. Taking him up on his offer," says Mum, not looking back.

"What offer? What do you mean?" I'm panting. This hill is killing me. Mum is way too fast.

"He's offered to let us stay with him," she says. She starts scrolling, looking for his number. She presses her phone to her ear.

"Stay with him? Mum! Get off the phone! We can't stay with Dimitri! We hardly know him!" I tug her sleeve, trying to get her to hang up.

She pulls away from me.

"Dimitri. Yes, it's me. Hi. Yeah, fine. Sorry I couldn't make it the other night."

"Mum!" I yell.

She silences me with a glare. Shoos me away.

"The camper's caved in. Disaster. I know. Awful place. Yes, oh that would be awesome. Yes, thanks, Dimitri."

"What? What's awesome? What are you saying?" I try to get closer to the phone so I can hear the other side of the conversation. I don't like the sound of what I'm hearing on this end.

"See you then. Thanks. Yes. Bye, Dimitri. Amazing. Yes, see you soon."

Mum hangs up.

"You just said we'd move in with him, didn't you?"
I ask. "Isn't that kinda unprofessional, for a real estate
agent to offer?"

Mum doesn't smile. She lifts an eyebrow.

"Dimitri's sweet, Queenie. You'll like him. I promise.
I know it's not in your nature, but please—just give him
a chance."

She trudges down the hill.

Again, I'm running after her. I twist my ankle when
my foot slides in the ditch.

The facts wobble in the stage wings. I know what
they are. I don't want to face them.

"You've been meeting up with him, haven't you?" I
say. "You've been meeting up with Dimitri behind my
back. The text messages. The smiley faces. You weren't
working the day before the flood. You were with
Dimitri."

Mum's sigh carries up the hill. At last she slows. She
turns.

"Yes, Queenie. Dimitri and I have gone on a couple
of dates."

It's worse than I thought.

"A couple?" I feel sick. I want to puke. Mum's been
having a secret life without me. A life with a man. A man
with shiny skin.

"How many's a couple?"

Mum sighs again. She looks away, then back at me. "Four times. The movies. Dinner. Lunch. Dinner. Okay?"

Not okay. So not okay.

I sprint back toward Ruthie's house, because the camper van's a goner. I slam the front door.

We're not going to Dimitri's. We're not moving in with some random real estate agent Mum likes.

I'm going to fix this.

I wish Ruthie was back so I could ask her if we can stay permanently in the main house. There's a guest room Ruthie keeps free for when her daughter comes to visit. We can stay there. I know it will be fine.

"What's up, Queenie?" asks Daisy when I push through her sarong door. She doesn't look up. She's lying on her bed studying for the GAMSAT, her ankles crossed in the air. Sonny's still not back, because of the causeway. But I don't mind. I've been liking having Daisy all to myself.

I slide onto the bed next to her. She still doesn't look up. She can't see my blotchy skin. The fight with Mum on my face.

"The camper's trashed. We can't live in it," I say.

"Uh-huh," says Daisy, one finger pressed to her book. She's wearing glasses that she doesn't usually wear. They make her look serious.

"Do you think Ruthie will let us stay in the spare room? We can stay somewhere else when Ruthie's daughter comes home."

Daisy's muttering something to herself as she reads. Instead of responding to my question, she says, "Hey, can you quiz me on this section?" She sits up, hands me her book, and points to a little gray box. "I have so much trouble with the periodic table. It's killing me."

The funny symbols jump around in front of me. Did Daisy really not hear what I said? Or is she just choosing not to respond?

"Can we, you think?" I ask. Pleading now. "I can stay and help you study. You can help me record my songs."

Daisy looks at the textbook in my hands, then up at me. She scrunches her nose, which pushes up her glasses.

"It's not up to me, Queenie. It's not my house. It's Ruthie's. I'm a tenant—just like you and your mum."

"But you can put in a good word for us!" I say. "Ruthie loves you!"

Daisy shrugs. "Look, Queenie. I'm just your substitute teacher who you happen to be sharing a property with for a bit. So the rain came and took the camper van away. It was never going to be a permanent solution." She takes the book out of my hands and plonks back on her tummy.

This conversation feels closed.

I won't lie—I'm hurt that Daisy isn't going to fight to keep me here with her. I thought we were friends. In some ways, other than Audrey—and Dory, I guess—Daisy is my first real friend in years. We had an actual connection.

Well, I thought we did.

I sit for a while. But Daisy doesn't say anything else. I finally get up and slip out of her room.

## twenty-eight

**WE DON'T HAVE LUGGAGE TO PACK.** So all that's left is
to wait for the causeway to go down. Mum checks the
progress every hour. Now that she's decided Dimitri is
the solution, she's desperate to get out of here.

Part of me hopes the causeway never goes down.

Another part of me can't wait. Since my conversation
with Daisy, things have been weird between us. I feel like
she's avoiding me. She doesn't come out to play music or
games. She's always in her room, either whispering on
the phone to Sonny or studying. She even takes her soup
to her room.

No one else seems to question it. But I know it's
because of me.

A day later, Ruthie comes back. Her four-wheel drive gushes through the causeway, so we hear her coming.

"Blimey," she says as she bustles into the kitchen. "That was touch and go!"

"How's the new baby?" I ask.

"Gorgeous," says Ruthie. "Mum and baby are a dream. Baby is feeding beautifully. And the mum was really happy to share her babymoon with her midwife."

"What's a babymoon?" I ask.

"Like a honeymoon. But after a baby is born, rather than after a wedding. A special time for the mum and baby to bond. Also keeps the illnesses away. Especially with all this COVID business. You can't be too safe."

I follow Ruthie between her car and the kitchen as she unpacks.

"Your mum okay? She seems a bit down-and-out," says Ruthie.

"The camper is ruined," I say. "I'm sorry, Ruthie. We tried to save it. But the roof was caving in on us."

To my surprise, Ruthie grins. "It's not worth the rent I was charging you. I'll give you a full refund. A piece of rubbish. You know I had that van when I was a kid, like you. Well, a bit older. Took it around Australia."

Relief rushes through me. I jump on Ruthie's generous mood.

Come on, words.

"Mum wants to move in with her boyfriend," I blurt out. The word catches. *Boyfriend.* "But we can stay here, can't we? We could rent the spare room, when your daughter's not here."

"Hm," says Ruthie. She bends and puts a big jar of kimchi in the fridge. "Nah. I need to keep that room free. I can't have other people in the main house. I need my personal space, you know?"

I'm stung. I really thought Ruthie would say yes. Beautiful, generous Ruthie, who shares meals every night because she likes company.

It's like Betsy kicking us out all over again.

The words race out of me before I have a chance to rein them in. "You don't understand. We have nowhere to go!"

I hurry out of the room and into the yard. I sit against the mulberry tree, which is over a hundred years old. Tears sting my cheeks.

# the fifth move
# DIMITRI'S PLACE

## twenty-nine

**OUR FAREWELL FROM SHOESTRING CREEK** is somber. Daisy does come out of her room, though, and hugs me. "Have a good Christmas!" she says. I realize my vague hopes of us hanging out are dashed.

Daisy is a schoolteacher, I remind myself.

She's not my friend.

Ruthie is friendly but preoccupied—she's preparing for another birth. Sonny's still away, and Xen doesn't bother coming to see us off. Only Tara squeezes my arm as if to keep me there.

"Don't go!" she says.

I hug her back and kiss her knotted hair.

Mum's little car gushes through the causeway, which is now covered only in a dirty film of water. We haven't spoken much since the phone call to Dimitri. I've been avoiding her. I can't get images of her and shiny-skin guy sitting side by side in the movie theater. Mum's betrayed me and she knows it.

But stuck here together for the next hour in the sardine can, there's no avoiding each other.

I open my window and let my fingers trail the rainforest air.

"Dimitri's a guitarist, you know," says Mum. I feel her eyes on me. I cringe. Of course he is.

"So?" I say. "I still don't want to live with him. I can't believe you've been lying to me all this time."

"I haven't been lying to you, Queenie. I just know how you can be."

Her words hurt. Mum shouldn't date. She's not ready. I'm not ready.

"You know moving in with your boyfriend is kind of taking things a bit fast, don't you?" I say.

"It's just a stopgap, Queenie. Till we find something of our own. We're not officially moving in."

This doesn't make me feel better. Especially when she doesn't contradict "boyfriend."

Curlew Point swallows us and feels comfortingly familiar after more than a week in the rainforest.

Everything looks so clean and civilized. I feel Mum overtly relax beside me.

So the rainforest wasn't her thing after all.

"What about Christmas?" I say. "It's only two days away."

"What about it?" Mum smiles, pleased that I am being nice to her for a moment.

"Can't we just do our usual? You and me? The Christmas market?"

The beachside Christmas market is every year on Christmas Day. It's like an orphans' Christmas, for people who don't have big families to spend Christmas with. There are lots of tourists and young people. But there might be fewer people this year, because COVID has made travel plans hard.

Before Gran disappeared to Toronto, the three of us would spend Christmas Day by the beach, eating pretzels and drinking hot chocolate. Now it's just Mum and me. Every year, I do my best to get Mum on the rides with me. She usually protests and then gives into one— like the carousel or something babyish. But I have never managed to convince her to go with me on my favorite ride—the Wild West. It looks and feels like a roller coaster that was made in someone's garage from spare parts. Mum's resistance might be sensible. But I know deep inside that she'll love the Wild West like I do, if she gives it a chance.

Mum reaches across and puts her hand on my knee.

"Christmas Day is all ours. Just you and me. I promise."

I can't help smiling.

We pull up in Dimitri's driveway. He's waiting for us, his shiny hair hanging over his eyes. He puffs to blow it away. "Here, let me take that for you, Queenie," he says, motioning to Garfield. His dimples are sickeningly deep.

"I'm fine," I say, pulling away. I plod behind Mum and Dimitri as we make our way up the hill. Dimitri's hill. I look over my shoulder. You can see the ocean from every angle.

Dimitri's place is "beach shack inspired," but it's anything but a shack.

We head through an archway of tropical plants and meander down a pebbly path. Surfboards are stacked against the side of the house. There are Balinese statues among the plants. A koi pond, with a fountain. I suck in my breath. After the rambling mess at Shoestring Creek, I swear this is Curlew Point's answer to Buckingham Palace.

"Beautiful place, Dimitri," says Mum.

I hate the way she looks up at him, all twinkling eyes.

"It's a bit over the top," I say under my breath but loud enough so both Dimitri and Mum hear me.

"Can you please remove your shoes?" asks Dimitri. "And keep the door closed so Frankie can't get out."

*Who's Frankie?* I wonder.

The living room is bathed in light. A huge flat-screen TV hangs on the wall in front of a modern square couch. A cowhide covers the stone floor.

"I'll show you your room, Queenie," says Dimitri.

I follow him down the hallway and up a set of stairs. My room—my very own room—has its own balcony, walk-in closet, bathroom, and a view of the swimming pool and the ocean.

Holy moly.

I make sure Dimitri doesn't see my smile. I stand in the middle of the room, not saying anything. Waiting for Dimitri to leave.

"Well—" says Dimitri finally. "I'll leave you to it, then. Feel free to use the pool whenever you like."

He heads to the door. I'm putting Garfield on the bedside table when Dimitri turns around.

"I hope you make yourself at home, Queenie. I want you to feel comfortable, yeah? *Mi casa, su casa.* My home, your home."

He closes the door. I exhale.

Home? Whatever.

I gaze over the ocean and see dolphins frolicking. You couldn't get a better view if you tried.

I lie on the bed, staring up at the ceiling. Garfield is beside me, cheery as ever. Somehow he manages to smile through everything.

But here I am in my own room, feeling . . . I don't know what. Empty?

This is it. My own room. All I've ever wanted since we left Peachy a month ago. But I can't help feeling as sparse as Dimitri's taste in furniture.

There's no warmth from the Diamonds dining room. Or a sun that spreads through your chest when the choir sings or when Audrey serenades her love.

There's no warmth of a lamp lighting up Dory's room in the dark as we draw together, side by side, and sing songs we made up.

There's no warmth from the fireplace while the rain drums down. The sound of music filling the scruffy rainforest kitchen.

Even though it's nearly Christmas and the beginning of summer, I feel cold.

And I miss Mum.

I miss the two of us.

At least I'll have her all to myself on Christmas. She's promised me that much.

Mum and Dimitri get takeaway for dinner. Mum comes to get me.

"Are you coming down?" she says. "We got Indian. Your favorite."

I can smell the garlic naan.

"Can I eat up here?" I say. "I have a headache."

Mum's mouth twitches. She wants to say no. She wants to tell me to come and be civil. But I think she still feels bad about springing this Dimitri thing on me.

Mum brings me a bowl, with a side of garlic naan.

"Hope your headache eases. I'll check on you later," she says.

"Can I have your phone?" I ask, trying to look like my head is throbbing.

I don't have a headache. I have a plan.

# thirty

**EVER SINCE WE LEFT PEACHY,** we've bounced around Curlew Point like a billiard ball. I realize now that it's all my fault.

I haven't been proactive enough. I've sat back and just let stuff happen to us. I wasn't paying enough attention and let Mum go off and get herself a live-in boyfriend. All because I've been thinking about myself.

I should have been doing more for us. For Mum and me. To keep us together. A family.

So now I have to get us out of this situation.

I scroll through Mum's Facebook app. I'm only twelve, so I'm technically not supposed to be on Facebook. But this is an emergency.

The "Living Life in Curlew Point" group is where I am headed.

There are loads more members than before. Over forty-four thousand now. That's a lot of people. And once again most of them are sincere smiling faces, pleading faces. "We need homes ASAP" faces.

Hi, Folks,

It's a week until Christmas, and me and my two boys are living in a van in a parking lot. All I want for Christmas is a home.

Please. Any leads, send me a DM.

Most Grateful xx

Hiya!

We're a couple just fresh up from Sydney. Totally chill. Vegans. Musicians. Happy to barter vegetables, gardening work, music lessons for rent.

Josie and Rudy

Hi,

My four upper-school-age kids and I have just been asked to leave our family home. We had a long-term lease, but it's been broken. And now we have nowhere to live. I am a single mum who works in care homes. It looks like if I don't find something soon, we are going to have to leave the region. I have a kid in their final year of upper school next year and they've been elected student president. I can't bear uprooting them at this stage of their life. Please help. Happy to pay whatever I can at this stage.

This last one makes my whole body ice over.

Mum and I might have to leave the area if this keeps going. This is what we are facing.

Maybe I should be grateful we have this mansion to live in. Even if it means sharing it with Dimitri, things could be so, so much worse.

I scroll through Mum's photos of us on her phone. There are loads, so it's hard to pick the best. But I choose one from two years ago. I look a bit different—my hair is still long. I'm more tanned. But it's definitely me. Mum looks the same.

We're on the steps of a shrine in Bali, on our last big trip together. It was Mum's thirtieth, and she treated us both to a two-week trip to Bali. We visited temples, ate nasi goreng, played with monkeys. It was the best trip I've ever been on.

Hi, friends,

We are a mum and daughter (age 12) looking for a home. We were asked to leave our forever home a month ago and are eager to put down roots again. I work in senior care, and my daughter's just finished grade school. We're respectful and caring and won't make a mess. We will love your home as our own.

I hesitate, wondering how people are going to contact us. Mum's going to go nuts when she starts getting random messages offering her a place to live.

*If* she starts getting random messages. There could be forty-four thousand people looking for homes right now.

Contact my friend Audrey, at Diamond Sands Seniors Village, Curlew Point.

I look up Audrey's number in Mum's address book and copy and paste it.

Post.

I throw Mum's phone on the bed and pick up Dad's guitar. I fingerpick my tune. Hum a little.

The song contest is in three weeks. Am I really going to get on a stage in front of strangers to play?

The thought of the stage and my inevitable flunk takes the magic out of my music session. I lie next to the guitar, wondering if I should go down and join Dimitri and Mum after all. At least there'd be conversation.

*Yip, yip.*

There's scratching at my bedroom door.

Is that . . .

a dog?

I open my door, and there's the cutest little teddy bear I have ever seen. His face is pure fluff. His little tongue sticks out. He leaps at me.

Dimitri has a puppy! OMG. This must be Frankie.

I grab the little guy and cuddle him. He licks all over my face. It's hilarious. I am so soggy, but I'm laughing my head off. He tries biting my fingers. His little teeth are sharp. But it's like being nibbled by coral.

Too cute. I love this little dude more than I've ever loved anything in my life.

Mum never let me get a dog. She said it was unfair leaving a dog at home alone for so many hours while she worked and I was at school. Also, vet bills.

I'm rolling around with Frankie on the floor when Mum comes by to pick up her phone. Thankfully, I've closed the Facebook app. I don't need to address that issue yet.

"So you've met Frankie!" she says. "I knew you'd love Frankie. You always wanted a dog!"

She laughs as Frankie bounds over my head over and over. He's making it impossible for me to get up. I grab him and wrestle him into a cuddle.

"Can I take him for a walk?" I ask.

"Ask Dimitri. But I'm sure he'd love that. Glad your head is feeling better."

## thirty-one

**WALKING FRANKIE IS NO EASY TASK.** He pulls so hard on the leash that I am sprinting to catch up. He has no idea about road safety, and I have to yank the leash to get him to stop at the road. When he stops every few minutes to sniff something or pee on something, I can't budge him at all.

I cringe when he poops right on someone's front lawn. I kneel to pick it up using the compostable bag Dimitri gave me. I try not to gag.

"Ew," says someone. "That's gross."

I look up.

Sparrow.

I hadn't recognized the house at first. The daylight is disappearing and the sky is peach. But now I see it's definitely Sparrow's house.

Of course it is.

I congratulate Frankie under my breath for his excellent taste.

"I never knew you had a dog," says Sparrow.

I hold the little poo bag by the knot. Pretty gross. But there has to be some cost for this much cuteness. If it means hanging out with Frankie, then I can hold a poo bag.

"I'm looking after him. His name is Frankie," I say.

Sparrow kneels and Frankie goes straight up to her. He licks her face and she, too, is laughing her head off. I realize I haven't seen Sparrow laugh properly since we were little kids. She's always so intent on presenting her übercool side at school.

Frankie springs between us, not sure who he wants to lick more. It's a lick fest. Sparrow and I can't stop giggling.

I could be sharing this moment with the devil, and Frankie would somehow manage to make it cute and fun.

But Sparrow isn't the devil. She's not even close. She just has a knack for choosing my favorite songs.

"Do you want to bring him out back and put him on the trampoline?" says Sparrow. "It'd be so cute."

I check my watch. It's getting late. Nearly bedtime. Dimitri might think I've stolen Frankie, which I have to say is pretty tempting.

"Okay. Just for a bit," I say.

"Oh, hi, Queenie! I hardly recognized you! You've gotten so tall!" Sparrow's mum, Lesley, pulls me into a familiar hug. I don't know why, but I feel myself welling up. She brings back all these memories . . . long afternoons just hanging out at the Hawkinses' house. Lesley making us popcorn. Jumping on the trampoline or swimming in the pool for hours and hours.

Sparrow and I sit cross-legged on the trampoline. Frankie swirls around between us. He keeps falling over. We die laughing. Lesley brings us popcorn, which we toss in the air for Frankie to try to catch. Then toss at each other. Like everything else in the world, Sparrow catches more popcorn than me. Then again, her mouth is huge.

"Your choir was pretty good," says Sparrow. "A big step up from last year! Every year, the Diamonds sing ye olde worlde songs. I can tell Granddad hates them. I swear he pretends to be more deaf than he actually is, so he can get out of choir."

"Yeah, it was pretty fun," I say. "I never thought about being a choirmaster. But I'm thinking of a career change."

Sparrow chuckles. "Are you still living with Daisy? Does she live near here?"

"Nope," I say. I don't elaborate. How could I tell Sparrow (of all people) that Daisy turned her back on me when I needed her most? "We're staying with one of Mum's friends, Dimitri. He has a pool and a huge TV. I have my own bathroom. And Frankie, of course."

Sparrow's smile is small. She gazes at Frankie, who's trying to lick the popcorn bowl clean.

"It must be nice having your own bathroom. And a dog. You're always so lucky, Queenie."

"I am?" I am legit taken aback right now. I stare at Sparrow. How on earth can she think I am lucky? Does she have any idea?

Does she have any idea what it's like to have a mum who has to head out for work at six o'clock every morning and is never able to take a sick day?

Or what it's like to make your own lunch and not know about things like checking lunch meat for the use-by date?

Doesn't she know what it's like to see your old best friend sing every song you wish you could, with confidence oozing out of every pore?

Or what it's like to lose your forever home and end up trekking around the north coast with no destination?

Doesn't she know what it's like to not have a real home for Christmas?

This Christmas, Sparrow will be hanging out in front of the Christmas tree with her whole family, opening presents, like every other year. COVID barely affects her. Life goes on.

Sparrow's holding Frankie now and trying to jump with him. Frankie, meanwhile, is trying to squiggle out of her arms.

"I better go," I say. "It's nearly dark. I don't want to get lost."

Sparrow walks me out to the front, carrying Frankie. She squeezes him hard and kisses his nose. "Aw, I'll miss you, Frankie! Bring him back tomorrow!" she says.

"Maybe," I say, and walk toward home. If you can call it that.

## thirty-two

**I DON'T PLAN ON TAKING FRANKIE BACK** to Sparrow's house straightaway. We've gone from strangers to friends in one evening. I'm not sure how I feel about this.

I do ask Dimitri, however, if I can take him to visit Audrey.

"He'll make her so happy!" I say.

Dimitri looks at Mum for an answer. She smiles and shrugs. "If you're okay with it, the village won't mind at all. They love animals. You just need to bring in the vaccination certificates for their records."

"I'll look after him!" I say.

Mum's not working, because it's Christmas Eve and she has a few days off. But she drives me in.

I hold Frankie behind my back and use my foot to push open Audrey's door.

"Merry Christmas!" I say. "I have a surprise for you!"

Audrey looks horrified when I put Frankie on her bed. "Get it off! Get it off!"

I am shocked by Audrey's response. I collect Frankie and hold him close. "How can you not like him?" I say.

"Didn't they tell you at reception? I have a dog allergy!" Immediately, Audrey starts sneezing. Her eyes are noticeably puffy.

"Oh, sorry, Audrey!" I say.

I lead Frankie back to the main building, where Mum's chatting with Meg, and get her to hold Frankie so I can hang out with Audrey without making her sick.

"I missed you," says Audrey. She wheezes. Her throat is still tight from all the sneezing. I feel bad.

"I missed you, too," I say. I fill Audrey in with everything—the flood, having to leave Shoestring Creek, Dimitri. I skim over the bits about Dory, but I can see her studying me.

"You like him, don't you?" she says.

I don't reply. Instead, I look out the window.

"Look at your cheeks! You're flushing! Well, if that's not a royal flush, I don't know what is! Have you serenaded him yet? I hear Sinatra works every time."

I grin. "As it happens, I have. But I only sing origi-nals these days. That way I know I am not going to be upstaged."

"You can't go wrong being original," says Audrey.

She tells me about the rom-coms she and Walter have been watching and about their plans for Christmas Day. Apparently, Diamonds is putting on a big lunch and everyone is dressing up. Since Audrey has no family to visit, she asks if I'll come by.

"Of course," I say, taking her hand. "By the way, has anyone called you about a house for us?"

"No? Why would they have?" Audrey narrows her eyes.

True. It's only been a day since I put up the post. "They might," I say.

Audrey's mouth moves into a serious line. "Now tell me about this Dimitri fellow your mum is seeing."

"There's not much to say. He has a big house. Big dim-ples. They're not really seeing each other. He's just help-ing us out of a tricky situation."

"Hm," says Audrey. "And if they were seeing each other? What does our cupid say about that?" She winks at me.

"Cupid?" I say.

"Yes, cupid. Matchmaker. You put me and Walter together. I imagine you're seeing the best in the situation for your mum's sake, at the very least."

Something ripples through me. I feel like Audrey is trying to teach me something, and I don't like it.

"I better get Frankie home. I'll come by tomorrow for Christmas," I say. "And I won't bring the dog."

## thirty-three

**I WAKE ON CHRISTMAS MORNING** with the usual Christmas buzz in my tummy. I may be twelve, but I go straight to the giant stocking I hung on the end of my bed. Dimitri has let Frankie sleep in my room, so Frankie is bouncing all over the bed and making it hard for me to look into my stocking.

Mum's gone all practical this year on account of us losing our stuff in the flood. Undies. Socks. Second-hand shorts and shirts. One brand-new T-shirt. It's a band T-shirt, but it's Metallica, which is not a band I listen to. I put the new clothes in the drawer beside my bed. Frankie meanwhile is tearing around my room with a pair of my new socks hanging out his mouth.

Gee, that dog makes me laugh.

Frankie and I trot down the stairs. I'm wearing the Metallica shirt and some Christmassy bauble earrings I made last year. I've bunched my hair together to make a topknot.

Mum smiles and pulls me in for a kiss. It's Christmas, and I am resolved to be Christmassy and kind. Also, Mum and I have the whole day together.

After breakfast.

"Thanks for the prezzies, Mum," I say.

"Love you, Queenie Pants," she says.

I hand Mum the little present I bought from the thrift shop and wrapped in some scrap paper. Mum lifts an eyebrow as she unwraps, then beams.

It's a tiny little gnome. Way prettier than Garfield.

Dimitri's not a Christmas tree guy. Unless you count the small wire statue thing on his steel kitchen counter. He's wearing an apron over his tailored shorts and is frying up a storm. I smell garlic. Immense amounts of garlic.

"A Russian-inspired feast. For my favorite ladies," he says, laying down the first dishes on the outdoor breakfast table. I try to focus on the calming sounds of the ocean below us so I don't end up hurling a garlic egg at Dimitri's dimpled face. I'm not anyone's "favorite lady."

Mum grins up at Dimitri appreciatively. "We're so lucky, aren't we, Queenie? Who could have imagined little old us would be spending Christmas Day like this?" She gestures to the ocean.

I poke the funny-colored food. The garlic tickles the back of my nostrils, it's so strong.

Mum and Dimitri chat easily about Christmases past and how Dimitri's family doesn't celebrate Christmas back in Russia. I cuddle Frankie and check my watch intermittently. I want to spend as much time with Mum at the Christmas market as I can.

"Queenie," says Dimitri from the other end of the table. "Christmas isn't on my radar, so I didn't get you a present in time. But it's coming, yeah? I know just the thing!" He winks at me.

Eek.

I start to clear the table in an attempt to hurry proceedings along. I need to escape.

"What a gem! So well-mannered. You raised her well, Clare," says Dimitri, patting my arm as I lift his plate. I pull away and take the plates to the dishwasher.

"Coming, Mum?" I say ten minutes later, my sunscreen and hat already on, my purse strapped across my tummy. I am giving Frankie cuddles before we head to the market.

"Where are you off to in such a hurry?" asks Dimitri from the breakfast table.

"Mum and I are going to the Christmas market. It's our tradition."

"Brilliant!" says Dimitri. "Let me grab my hat. I love that market."

I stare at Mum. Why isn't she saying anything?

"Sorry, Dimitri," I say. "It's kinda just for Mum and me. Like, the two of us. Come on, Mum."

"Oh," says Dimitri. He looks like I just kicked him in the shins. "That's fine, I guess. I just thought we were hanging out."

Mum's eyes are pleading with me from across the living room.

*Come on, Queenie*, I hear her say. *Be nice.*

"Fine," I mutter. "You can come. I suppose."

Dimitri grins like a four-year-old. He grabs a poo bag and stuffs it in his pocket. "It'll be a good old-fashioned family outing! Love it!" he says.

I scowl over at Mum. All she can offer is a grateful shrug.

The only consolation is that now Frankie is coming along with us.

## thirty-four

**WE PARK UNDER A BIG NØRFØLK PINE,** and Dimitri winds down the windows a bit.

"Frankie has to stay in the car," says Dimitri just as I am clipping on Frankie's leash.

"What? Why? That's so cruel. It's Christmas! And it's way too hot to leave him here."

"No dogs allowed," says Dimitri, pointing to the oversize NO DOGS sign hanging on the fence.

Dimitri locks the Land Rover and throws me his car keys. "How about you come out every half hour and check on Frankie? Give him a drink and let him stretch his legs."

I pocket the keys and stick my hand through the window to give Frankie a farewell pat.

I plod through the Christmas beachside market at

a safe distance from Mum and Dimitri. At some point, Dimitri reaches toward Mum and grabs her hand.

My Christmas is officially broken.

I nibble my stupid pretzel.

I wander around on my own for a bit. I see a few kids from school on rides. One waves. I wave back and retreat into the shade next to the bathrooms, watching Mum and Dimitri line up for coffee. Mum's laughing, her head thrown back. Dimitri is feeding her potato on a stick.

"You don't look like you're having the best day," says someone, sinking to the ground next to me.

"Huh?" My neck cracks, I turn so fast. Dory has a stripe of sunscreen on his nose that he hasn't rubbed in properly.

An ocean fills me from the head down.

"Oh, hi, Dory," I manage.

"So what's the story, Morning Glory? Did Santa miss your house this year?" Dory's expression is caring but light-humored.

"Huh. Nope. Santa came. Brought me a lovely T-shirt. See?" I pluck the front of my Metallica shirt.

Dory grins. "Didn't pick you for a Metallica fan."

I lift one shoulder. "Well, you know—I'm not really. But, hey. If Santa wants me to get into Metallica, then I guess I can do that for him. What did Santa bring you?"

Dory shows me his watch. It's slick and black, with all kinds of knobs. "It's so I can time my games," he says.

Dory the chess wizard.

"How'd you do at the competition?" I ask.

"Really good!" says Dory. "I got to the grand finals! But I was beaten by Sara Romkoff. She's amazing."

Sara Romkoff, the amazing chess player. I dislike her very much already. After my dismal chess performance in Dory's room, I know chess will never be the thing that brings me and Dory closer.

"Cool!" I say, trying to look happy for Dory.

"Oh, I have a Christmas present for you!" says Dory.

"You do?" I blush. I feel bad I haven't gotten anything for Dory. How did he know we'd even see each other today?

He pulls out a phone. I never thought Dory would be the type of kid to have a phone. He seems so wholesome. But like me, Dory's an only child. I know lots of only kids get phones earlier than other people so they can call their parents if they get stuck somewhere. And they've always got something to do when they are by themselves.

He opens Spotify, types something into search, and presses play. I bite my lip, listening, as he holds the speaker up to my ear. I can't believe what I'm hearing.

"It's my song," I say under my breath.

Dory's looking at me quizzically. I can see he's nervous.

It's not the whole song, because I haven't played the entire thing for him yet. And the recording is pretty average, given that Dory just used the headset microphone he uses for gaming, and nothing pro that you'd usually use to record music.

Still.

Something fills me, from the shins up. I don't know this feeling. It's like my body is being turned inside out and is changing shape. I'm becoming someone else. I'm listening to such a big part of myself that used to be inside and is now walking around in the world, without me. All grown up.

The song finishes. Dory puts his phone in his pocket. His eyebrows are raised.

"Happy Christmas?" he says.

"Thanks," I say. I feel my cheeks burn hard.

"You're mad at me," he says.

I grab his skinny wrist. The one without the watch. "No! I'm not. I'm just . . . I don't know how I feel, if I'm honest. It's weird, hearing my song played back to me."

"I shouldn't have posted it without your permission, it's just—it's . . . well, it's so good, Queenie. I'm really proud of you. And look!" He pulls the phone out again and reopens the app. "You already have eighteen followers, just for that one song!"

I'm pretty shocked by that. Who are these eighteen people? Eighteen random people somewhere in the world are listening to my song.

"I'm happy you did it," I say finally. I realize as I say it that I am happy. I would never have had the guts to share my music online like that. But hearing it with its big-girl pants on is a pretty cool thing.

"Dory Elliot!" I peek around the corner of the bathrooms. Sure enough, Maggie is striding toward us. I gulp.

"Sorry, Dory, I don't want you to get in trouble again! I don't think I can face Maggie today. Happy Christmas!"

I squeeze his hand. I'm about to run off, but Dory is holding my wrist.

"What are you doing?" I ask. He's writing something on the inside of my arm in pen.

"My email address," he says quickly before rushing over to meet his mum. I disappear into the restrooms to hide from her.

After counting to a thousand, I decide that I'm being silly about Mum and Dimitri. Dimitri can come to the Christmas market if he wants to. They can hold hands if they have to, I suppose. Seeing Dory and hearing my song on Spotify has reset my head.

I am going to be a good daughter and a good person. I am going to be Christmassy and cheery.

And I am going to get Mum on the Wild West ride with me if it's the last thing I do. She owes me that at least.

I check the coffee stand, where I last saw Mum and Dimitri. I walk past the carnival games. A tall girl with red dreadlocks throws a hoop that goes straight onto a hook. The crowd cheers. The guy reluctantly passes her a stuffed Mr. Potato Head.

A Santa with his pant legs rolled up is handing out candy to kids from a sack.

"Ho, ho, ho!" he says, wiping sweat from his brow. The kids stick their grubby hands in the bag, pushing each other aside to get more candy than the person next to them.

It's Christmas anarchy.

I finally spot Mum and Dimitri. They're in another line. Dimitri puts his hand on Mum's back. Something in me fizzes.

The ride attendant opens the gates. Mum's laughing at something clearly hysterical. She and Dimitri walk through the gates and climb into a Wild West carriage.

The fizz rushes through me. My tummy constricts.

"Mum!" I call out over the rail. I wave. But she doesn't see me. She doesn't hear me. She's only got eyes and ears for Dimitri.

And they're doing the ride without me. The ride Mum never goes on, even when I plead with puppy-dog eyes.

That's it. I'm out. This Christmas is officially over. The only creature who can save me now is Frankie.

## thirty-five

**FRANKIE'S NOSE AND TONGUE ARE HANGING OUT** the tiny gap in the window. The poor little guy is frying. I unlock the door, and Frankie bounds toward me. I pull him into a slobbery hug. I lock Dimitri's fancy-pants car and stick the keys deep in my pocket. Can't have anyone breaking in, now, can we?

I give Frankie the last of the water in my bottle. Because it's so hot and we are both baking, I decide to take Frankie to the beach. Part of me hopes that the sea breeze and salty water will wash my bad Christmas juju away.

Frankie runs straight into the water, then disappears under a wave. I'm fully dressed but throw Dimitri's car keys in my hat on the sand and race into the water. I get to Frankie right before another wave pulls him under. Frankie emerges, panicked. He looks like a drowned rat. He scrabbles frantically, trying to find solid ground.

I rescue him from the big bad scary ocean, laughing at the funny little bedraggled thing he's become. We roll around on the sand for a bit, Frankie nibbling my chin. Sand is wedged in every crevice. At some point, I spit out a mouthful.

Frankie, sand, and salty water. This is everything I didn't know I ever needed. I figure I'll spend the rest of Christmas here with Frankie.

He understands. He makes me feel more like myself again.

After ten minutes or so of playing on the sand, I'm desperate for shade and I bet Frankie is, too. We bound through the scrublands. Dogs probably definitely are not allowed here, so I am praying we don't see a ranger. Or they don't see us. Luckily Frankie and I are quick.

I leash Frankie once we get to the play park because there are lots of kids around. He can't contain himself. Every kid is a bouncy house as far as Frankie is concerned.

I suddenly remember Audrey and my promise to come visit her on Christmas Day.

Mum is busy with Dimitri. She doesn't have time for Frankie or me. Why would she have time for Audrey?

Frankie and I are going to see Audrey. Well, I am anyway. Frankie can hang out in the Diamonds reception for a bit.

It's lucky the market is beachside, so I have a reference point. I follow the beach for a bit before Frankie and I dart into town. I wind down one of the streets and recognize the IGA supermarket. I know it's not far from Diamonds. My spirits lift.

But a street or two later, I am lost. I don't have a phone or any sense of direction.

I recognize a blue house—it's one we always pass on the way to Mum's work. I'm sure it is. I march up the street, confident now that I am completely on track.

But it must have been a different blue house. Or maybe I took the wrong street.

There is no Diamond Sands Seniors Village anywhere.

My throat is scratchy with thirst. My legs ache. Sweat trickles from every pore. Frankie pulls me under a poinciana tree and plonks in the grass, panting hard.

Even Frankie the Energizer Bunny is spent.

I sprawl on the grass next to Frankie, to try to restore some energy.

I check my watch. I probably left the Christmas market an hour ago. Mum and Dimitri must be starting to freak out. Dimitri will think I've stolen his dog and his keys.

Mum will think I've been stolen.

No one will expect that I ran away in a little twelve-year-old tizzy because my mum rode a roller coaster without me, and then got hopelessly lost because I suck at directions. If only I'd paid more attention all those times Mum and I drove to Diamonds. It can't be rocket science. Curlew Point isn't a huge city or anything.

*I could ask someone. If I can just get to Diamonds, Mum will be able to find me. Meg or whoever is working will call her. Frankie and I will be okay.*

There's a family gathered around a dining room table in the house we are sitting in front of. I see them through the big window and hear their voices rise and fall as I knock on the door.

The man who answers has gravy on his shirt.

"Um, sorry to disturb you. My name is Queenie. I am just wondering if you know where Diamond Sands Seniors Village is?"

The man squints and shrugs. "No. No, sorry. I don't." He calls over his shoulder. "Does anyone know where Diamond Sands Seniors Village is?"

"The old people's home?" someone calls back.

"Yes," I call over gravy man's shoulder.

"Other side of town, dear," I hear someone say.

How could I have gotten it so wrong?

I thank the man and leave before anyone can ask any more questions. I'm halfway down the block before it occurs to me that I should have at least asked for a glass of water.

∘ ∘ ∘

The sun is definitely easing. It's less glary but still hot. I'm carrying Frankie now. The poor thing must be so dehydrated. I know I am. I keep seeing stars and feel like I am going to black out. But I march on, determined to find the Christmas market again. The IGA. The beach! Anything I know or recognize.

Another part of me wants to stay lost forever. Mainly because when Dimitri sees me, he's going to be so mad I stole his precious dog and his car keys. He won't trust me anymore. Just like when I broke Maggie's trust, he'll toss us out, because why would he be so hospitable to a little thief?

There's a faucet on the outside wall of some public bathrooms. I feel like crying as I wrench it on. It's so stuck. Eventually, the faucet turns and water spurts everywhere. Frankie's so weak, he can barely be bothered to lick the water. But I'm throwing it on my face, then cupping my hands to drink. I hold my cupped hands under Frankie's mouth.

"Come on, boy. Drink!" I plead. I lift my hands so his nose submerges in the water. He finally licks the water. His tongue gets quicker and quicker as his energy returns.

I sink against the side of the building and rest my head on my knees. My whole body aches. I pull Frankie into my chest and let myself cry into his fur.

I'm so stupid.

How could I have gotten myself so lost?

I let my eyes close. Just for a bit. I need to rest before we keep going. Not long. Just a tiny moment. Not long at all.

# thirty-six

**"QUEENIE ANDERSON?"**

I'm being shaken.

I wake, bleary-eyed. The sky is softer now. The sun is low in the sky. A policewoman stands over me. She's wearing Ray-Bans on her head. A radio is cradled between her head and her shoulder.

"Found 'em, over," she says into the radio. It crackles in reply. She crouches next to me and holds out a bottle of water. I realize there's a second police officer behind her. A tall guy wearing a cap. He's a dark silhouette against the setting sun.

"Drink up," says the female officer. "Your lips are cracked. You must be dehydrated."

I drink noisily. When I wipe my mouth, my lips sting.

"Where's Mum?" I ask.

"She's at the station. Jason and I'll give you a lift now."

"Do you have water for Frankie, too?" I ask.

She smiles and pulls a little bottle from her belt. "Sure do. Here, li'l fella." She tips the water into her hand. Frankie laps it dry.

I don't talk in the police car. I don't know what to say. Who to thank. How to explain.

I feel sick about seeing Mum and Dimitri. They're going to be so mad.

Mum's hunched over in one of the gray plastic chairs in the waiting room. Dimitri's hand is on her back again. But it's a different montage now. There's no laughing. No fairground rides.

Mum's face explodes with relief when she sees me. She runs to me. I bury myself in her smell. She's all pretzels and sunscreen, and I have never loved anyone more in my life.

After forever, Mum holds me at arm's length. I stiffen, waiting for her to yell at me. But she just looks at me, her face tearstained, before pulling me in for another hug.

"We were so worried," she says, her voice crackly. "There's a whole lot of people out looking for you.

Dimitri and I looked and looked—" She stops, unable to keep going.

Dimitri hangs back. I let Frankie go. Frankie runs to Dimitri, who bundles him up. Frankie licks Dimitri's face.

"So, so glad you two are okay," he says to me.

I'm surprised. His voice is warm. Kind, even. When he looks at me, his eyes, too, are swimming in tears.

I'd expected him to disown us. But instead he's pleased to see me.

It's disarming.

"I'm sorry," I say. I hold out Dimitri's car keys. It takes him a moment, but he plucks them out of my hand.

"I'm just so relieved you're okay, Queenie. Your mum and I thought the worst, we really did. That ocean is endless, you know. So dangerous."

Guilt tugs at my insides.

How could I have been so selfish? Mum and Dimitri would have imagined all sorts of things. Me and Frankie drifting out to sea, never to be found again would have probably been the first thing.

"Thank you, Constable Mason," Mum says over my shoulder. When Mum smiles at me, her eyes well up all over again.

"Never do that to me again," she says into my hair. "You're my Queenie Pants—you know that, right? I can't function without you."

"I'm sorry, Mum," I say. And I really mean it.

## thirty-seven

**DIMITRI SAYS HE CAN'T FACE COOKING TONIGHT.** He has to drive twenty minutes to pick up a roast chicken from the big supermarket in Ravensdale because everything is closed in Curlew Point.

We eat quietly at the porch table, using our fingers to pick at the chicken. The mayonnaise makes funny noises when it squirts out of the bottle.

Cockatoos swarm the lawn in front of Dimitri's place. Their incessant chatter fills the evening air.

"I'm sorry again," I say over the birdcalls. "I didn't mean to steal your dog and your keys, Dimitri."

To my surprise, Dimitri grins. "We've all done it," he says, chuckling. I must look surprised, because he elaborates. "When I was fourteen, I drove my mum's car into a wall. You're doing fine, Queenie."

He hands me the salad bowl without my even asking for it.

Dimitri might have a fancy house, and he might like my mum in ways that don't sit comfortably with me . . . yet. But he's not terrible. In fact, he's really sweet about this whole thing. Another person might have blown up at me. Kicked us out. Sent us on our way.

But not Dimitri. Instead he drove to Ravensdale to buy roast chicken.

"Oh, I nearly forgot! Your present! I picked it up from my friend Harry's on my way back. Just a sec."

He jogs out to the garage and returns with something behind his back. It's big, and I can see already what it might be.

My breath catches.

He presents an electric guitar.

It's vintage—I can tell. It's a Fender Stratocaster with dark wood and a cream center. I gasp, clutching it. It's so heavy, I nearly drop it through Dimitri's glass table.

"I—wow. Thank you. Are you sure? These are expensive."

Dimitri shrugs, grinning. "I've had it for years and never played it. It feels selfish, keeping it for myself.

I lent it to Harry for a while, but now that he's got little kids, he doesn't have time for the band. It's time it had a new home. Someone to love it."

Mum's smiling between me and Dimitri. I pull the strings. They're so light compared to what I am used to.

I've never played electric. Only ever Dad's old acoustic. But I'll take anything that makes music.

A wave passes through me.

This means Mum told Dimitri that I play. It feels like Dimitri knows something really private about me. Knowledge he should earn.

But maybe he has earned this.

Maybe I can let him in.

# thirty-eight

**AFTER DINNER, I PLAY TO THEM BOTH** for a bit. I don't have an amp, so it sounds tinny. When we sing "Silent Night" together, it doesn't matter that I'm not amped up. Dimitri surprises me with his beautiful tenor voice.

Dimitri excuses himself to call his family in Russia from the study. Mum and I watch *Love Actually* on the modern sofa. Frankie's cuddled up between us. We watch this movie pretty much every Christmas. But this is the first time we've watched it on a ginormous high-definition TV with surround sound. It feels like we are inside the film.

Mum's crying way more than usual when Emma Thompson's character opens up her Joni Mitchell CD and realizes her husband is cheating on her. She's a blubbering mess when Colin Firth's character proclaims his love to Aurelia in broken Portuguese.

I put my arm around Mum. She makes my T-shirt soggy.

"It's been a weird month, Queenie. I know it hasn't been easy on you," she says.

"I haven't been easy on you," I say. "I shouldn't have gone off like that."

"It was scary," Mum admits.

I want to tell her why. I want her to know that I didn't just get lost by accident. That I really wanted to get away.

"You went on the Wild West ride without me. With Dimitri," I say. "That hurt. You never want to do that ride with me. Anyway, I thought the Christmas market was supposed to be you and me. Our day. Just for us."

Mum's lips squeeze together. She wipes away a stripe of mascara from the side of her face.

"You're right, Queenie. I abandoned you on one of the most important days of the year. I'm really sorry, baby. I guess I'm . . ." Her look wanders away, as if she's thinking of the right words to choose.

"You like Dimitri. I get it. Maybe you like Dimitri more than a friend," I say.

Mum's gaze returns and rests on me. She takes both my hands in hers. Frankie nuzzles in, not wanting to be forgotten.

"Maybe," she says. "Would that be so bad, Queenie Jean? How would you feel if I *like* like Dimitri?"

I stay quiet.

I've known for a few days now that Mum *like* likes Dimitri.

I've never wanted her to have a new boyfriend. Maybe a grown-up part of me does—the part of myself I'd like to be. The Queenie who can stand onstage with a Fender and sing her own music to a crowd of strangers.

But the bigger part of me—the little Queenie part—wants to keep Mum to myself forever. Her and me and Peachy, just like it always was.

But Peachy's not there anymore. And Mum's changing. Maybe I am, too.

"I don't mind," I say finally. "Dimitri is kind."

As I say it, I know it's true. Dimitri is kind. Shouldn't that be all that matters?

o o o

It's almost midnight and I'm brushing my teeth. I grin, seeing Dory's email address scrawled on my arm.

Dimitri's in his room. Mum's in the guest room. I tiptoe to the study. Dimitri's computer is still on.

I open Gmail and sign in.

To: Dory E.
From: Queenie Jean
Subject: Thank you
Hi, Dory,
I liked seeing you today.

Thank you for recording my song. It was weird hearing it on Spotify. But good weird. The way new jeans feel weird and too tight, but you know they are going to be perfect after a few wears.

Happy Christmas :)
Queenie

## thirty-nine

**THE LAST WEEK OF DECEMBER AND THE START** of January are spent swimming in Dimitri's pool, playing with Frankie, walking Frankie, playing my song, writing new songs, and even visiting Sparrow.

At first, I only stay ten minutes at Sparrow's, so she can see Frankie. But our visits have gotten longer. Last Tuesday, Frankie and I spent the whole day in Sparrow's backyard. It's almost like when Sparrow and I were in kindergarten. Except now we have a dog and are about to start at the upper school.

Dory and I are emailing most days, too.

My chest feels tight every time I go to check Gmail.

Dory's emails are short and funny. He pretty much always links to random articles, like articles about the last female Swinhoe's turtle that died in 2019, leaving the last male Swinhoe's without a mate. Apparently, researchers have just found another female Swinhoe's though, which means the oldest turtle species in the world might not end up being extinct after all.

I send Dory snippets of my songs, which I record on Mum's phone. He writes back with lots of smiley face emojis, which give me lots of inside smiley faces every time.

The days Mum works, I try to see Audrey. Usually, Mum drives in early for her shift at Diamonds and Dimitri keeps an eye on me until he has to go to work. Then Frankie and I take the bus to Diamonds until Mum finishes. Frankie hangs out with Meg, who takes him around to the residents on her rounds. He's become the favorite part of every resident's day. Every resident except Audrey, that is.

"So, have you had any messages about a house for Mum and me?" I ask Audrey one afternoon. Mum's due to knock off in about thirty minutes. Audrey and I have finished her daily crossword and *Dirty Dancing*.

I ask Audrey every visit if she's heard anything. Always, the answer is no.

I don't mind Dimitri's. If I am truly honest, I kind of like it. I'm getting used to having a pool and my own room and bathroom. And Frankie is the best thing that ever happened to me.

But it kind of feels like Mum and I are living in a hotel. A time-being hotel. Waiting on the edge of reality. Even though I'll miss the perks, I want Mum and me to have our own place. Just the two of us again. My own wall to destroy with Blu-Tack. My own stuff. My own place to make music and just be me, no questions asked.

"I told you, Queenie, I'm not your secretary," says Audrey.

"Yes, but Mum can't know I posted about us on social media. She feels like it's begging. It's not. But I don't want to make her mad."

"She'll find out eventually," says Audrey. "I don't think you've thought this through."

"Are you sure you haven't had any messages? Do you even check your voicemail?"

"'Course I do!" she says defensively.

But there's a light flashing on Audrey's answering machine.

"What's that?" I ask.

Audrey shrugs. "No idea."

"Audrey!" I jump up and press play. Wow, the wonders of modern technology. The answering machine crackles to life. The voice sounds like it belongs to someone who has drunk a lot of whiskey and smoked a lot of cigarettes.

"Hello, Audrey, this is Wesley Smith. We used to work together at Butterby's. Do you remember? I heard you were living at Diamond Sands. That's wonderful! I'm over at Rosemary Hedge up at Williams Head. I just wondered if you wanted to meet up for a drink one night. Lots to catch up on! Give Rosemary Hedge a call, and ask for Wesley. Their number's in the phone book."

I raise my eyebrows at Audrey. "Is there something you're not telling me? What about Walter?"

"Walter has nothing to worry about!" says Audrey in indignation. "Wesley is an old, old beau. I barely remember him! How on earth he heard I was at Diamonds, I'll be darned! What else is on that thing?"

She points a crooked finger at the answering machine. The light's still flashing. I press play again.

"Hello? This is a message for—" The voice cuts out, and the machine beeps.

"Anything else?" asks Audrey.

I press play again. The same voice starts again. It sounds like a younger person. A woman.

"Hello, this is a message for Clare Anderson. Sorry, I hope I have the right number. I saw your post on

Friday, and I am looking for someone to house-sit while I look after my sick dad in Victoria. Please call me if you are still looking for a place to stay." Then she leaves her number.

The light stops flashing. I press replay, my heart beating fast as I write down the number.

"How long has that light been flashing?" I ask. Friday could have been last Friday or the Friday before. In fact, I think there have been three Fridays since I posted the message in the Facebook group.

Audrey shrugs. "How should I know?"

"Can I use your phone?" I say.

I call the number. A lady picks up on the third ring.

"Hello?" she says.

"Hello, this is . . ." I clear my throat. "Clare Anderson."

Audrey grabs my wrist too hard. She's shaking her head. But I am already on the train, and there's no getting off. "I'm sorry, I only just got your message about needing a house sitter. Do you still need one? We're interested."

The lady is quiet. I'm not sure if she's still there. "Hello?" I say.

"Sorry," she says. "I have to go. I have to get to my dad's funeral. Thanks for your call. But I sorted out something with the house."

The phone cuts off. I hold the handset, as if waiting for it to do something.

"I take it that's a no," says Audrey.

I nod. "Yes. I mean, you're right. It's a no."

I feel awful for the poor lady. I don't remember losing my dad. But I can imagine . . .

"Just as well, then," says Audrey. "Your mum would have flipped her lid to know you're going behind her back."

My tummy knots up. Audrey's right. I need to tell Mum about the Facebook post. Big-girl pants and all that.

# forty

**AS LUCK WOULD HAVE IT, I DON'T GET TO CHOOSE.** Mum got a Facebook message while she was working, asking if she was still looking for a home, and did she want to check out a shared house in Shoestring Creek?

"Queenie, do you know anything about this?" she says, showing me the message when we get in the car.

I pull Frankie to my chest for moral support. I need to come clean before this escalates.

"I posted a message," I say. "I just thought—"

Mum sighs. She starts the car. "Queenie, you can't do stuff like that. You have to talk to me. What was your plan exactly?"

I shrug and look at the dashboard. "I guess I was hoping to find us a place," I say quietly.

"I thought you liked Dimitri's. You look like you're having the time of your life floating in his pool with your mocktails."

"It's fine," I say. "But it isn't ours."

Mum nods. I sneak a glance to read her expression. She doesn't look too mad, which is a good thing.

"Shoestring Creek is not for us," she says. "Anyway, I have a bit of news. I didn't want to say anything, in case it falls through. But Dimitri might have found us a place."

"What?" I spin to face her. "You're joking, right? A place of our own?"

Mum grins. "Maybe. But don't get your hopes up, Queenie! You know things are tough right now. Very competitive and all that. Dimitri can't be seen to be doing too many favors. But he can put in a good word for us. It all helps."

"What's the place like?" I say. "Can we drive past?"

Mum sighs. But she's smiling.

"Fine. We can drive past."

The place is in a gated community, not far from the beach. A sign reading HERITAGE GARDENS hangs on the gate.

"It looks like a retirement village," I say. Still, I am pretty excited. The thought of our own place is making me giddy. I can stick up my posters. And not have to share Mum with anyone. I can play my music at full volume. Or maybe not, if it's a retirement village.

Mum laughs.

"It's not a retirement village. It's a gated community. Not our usual fare. But there's a two-bedroom place available. Tiled floor. Easy to maintain. No mowing." She pumps her fist. Mum always hated mowing Betsy's lawn in the heat.

"And it'll be ours," I say. "Can we walk around?"

Mum shakes her head. "It's a gated community for a reason. We'll find out tomorrow maybe if our application is successful. They've already called our references."

"I can't believe you've been keeping this from me!" I say.

o o o

We don't find out tomorrow. By the end of the day, Mum's back to scratching her eczema.

"We can watch *You've Got Mail*," I say after dinner, eager to distract her. "We haven't seen it in eleven years."

"Actually, Queenie," says Dimitri, "I was hoping to show you something."

Mum and I exchange a look.

I follow Dimitri into his garage. It no longer contains his Land Rover. Beside Dimitri's impressive array of camping gear is a giant cardboard box.

"Um," I say, staring at the cardboard thing. "Should I open it or something?"

"You should go *in* it or something!" says Dimitri. I swear he's like a little kid sometimes.

I creep around the perimeter of the box. On the other side is a door. I open it and go inside. It's a little cardboard room with a chair, a computer, and a mic.

"It's a recording studio!" says Dimitri from outside the box. "My friend Harry helped me set it up this afternoon. He created one of these in lockdown so he could keep doing his podcast. Neat, hey?"

I plonk into the chair, speechless.

Dimitri made all this for me? When I picture his beloved Land Rover parked out on the curb, I think I might cry.

"Thank you," I say, hoping my words make it through the soundproof walls.

## forty-one

**I LOG ON TO SPOTIFY THE NEXT MORNING,** using the log-in details Dory emailed me. There I am. A new portrait of me that Dory's drawn in pencil. I'm holding a guitar, looking down.

Queenie Jean is the name of the account. And Queenie Jean now has 104 followers, even though she's only ever posted half a song. Dory says my song is on a Mood playlist, which means it gets loads of listens. It's still called TBA, which listeners might think is meant to be ironic but is actually literal. The song's title is still to be announced.

This song needs to be announced. And so do all my other songs I've written this summer.

I don't have Logic Pro, so Dory has told me to record into GarageBand, which is the app that comes with the computer.

In my little cardboard studio in Dimitri's garage, I play take after take of "Summer Home" and my other tracks. First the guitar, then the vocals.

When I am satisfied with the recordings of my three songs, I Dropbox them to Dory. He emails me back within about ten minutes.

To: Queenie Jean
From: Dory E.
Subject: Holy WOW!
Queenie! You are a teen sensation! I am transferring the files into Logic as we speak. Give me 24 hours. I will upload to Spotify. Then let's watch the magic roll out.
D.
P.S. Do you think I can come check out your recording studio when I'm done?

*o o o*

Three days later, Dory and I are cramped together on the chair in my recording studio. I wear my headphones, listening to my tracks on Spotify. Dory's grinning at me literally the whole time.

I won't lie. My songs fill me with—what's the word? Pride? They might not be Billie Eilish. But they are Queenie Jean, and holy moly, that girl is not bad for a twelve-year-old.

I hug Dory hard when I finish.

"So good, right?" he says.

"You did an amazing job on the bass," I say. "Sounds really cool in 'Victory' especially. Can't believe you taught yourself all that from YouTube!"

"Can't believe you taught *yourself* all that from YouTube!" He chuckles. "You are so ready for the Summer Song Contest. Isn't it next week or something?"

The buzz seeps out my earholes. "Oh," I say. "I'm not going."

"What? Why? You have to go! You have fans, silly! You can't let them down!"

"I am sure the hundred and four followers in China or Poland or wherever they are will survive if I bail on Saturday," I say.

"That's not the point," says Dory. "Bailing is for losers."

"Ouch," I say. His words are sewing needles stabbing me in my arm. "I told you I bailed at the Christmas concert. And the end-of-year concert. You think I'm a loser?"

Dory pulls his mouth into a tight line. I feel heat ripple through me. I throw open the cardboard door, no longer able to bear sharing oxygen with my so-called friend Dory Elliot, who thinks I am a loser.

I march out of the garage. Frankie's waiting for me at the garage door and leaps into my arms, licking my face.

"Care for a walk, fluff-face?" I say, clicking on his leash. "I need fresh air."

I walk and walk. Nowhere and anywhere. For some reason, I find myself at Sparrow's.

I suppose Sparrow is my only other friend, unless you count Audrey. Which I do.

Sparrow's on the porch, cutting her toenails. She launches at Frankie and twirls him around like a stuffed toy. Frankie so does not mind. He's doing his best to lick her to death.

"Trampoline time!" she cries.

I perch on the swing while Sparrow bounces.

"You look glum," says Sparrow, finally noticing that I'm not joining in the Frankie fun.

"Dory called me a loser," I say.

"Ouch," says Sparrow.

"That's what I said."

"Don't hang out with him if he's going to treat you like that," says Sparrow. "You shouldn't be friends with bullies."

"Dory isn't a bully," I say. "He probably didn't mean it. He was just trying to get me not to bail on the song contest."

"What song contest?" says Sparrow.

Uh-oh. I've blown it now. The secret is out.

"It's nothing," I say, waving it away. But I know Sparrow will be on Google seconds after I leave, finding out everything she needs to know to upstage me at the Summer Song Contest. Reason number 625 why I won't be performing there on Saturday.

Sparrow plays her cards well and refrains from mentioning the Summer Song Contest while she bounces with Frankie.

o o o

I'm in my room at Dimitri's house relistening to my songs. I have 118 followers now. Apparently, a few extra people came on board since Dory uploaded my new songs.

I'm lying there with a big fat smile on my face. I can't help it. It sounds conceited. But I genuinely love my songs. If anyone else had made them, I would have followed and liked them like crazy.

But *I* made them.

Well, me and Dory.

Dory's Logic Pro skills are beyond belief. The guy can play chess, draw like a fiend, and mix music like a pro.

Mr. Grey would be proud of me.

Daisy would be proud of me.

I'm proud of myself.

I don't care about my fans in Poland or wherever. But I do care about the fan lying with Frankie in Dimitri's house listening to her own songs on Spotify. I actually care a lot about that fan: Queenie Jean.

Which is why I am going to go to the Summer Song Contest.

*o o o*

Williams Head is two and a half hours away. We could potentially drive up and back in one day, but Mum wants to make a trip out of it.

"I'm going on Airbnb!" she says. "I am so excited about this, you have no idea."

But moments later, her face falls. "Pity I am not a millionaire. Can you believe this place? They want five hundred and fifty dollars for one night!" She taps her phone. "It's not even that nice!"

I think of Dimitri's camping gear in the garage. It's a long shot. Mum's not a camper. She's barely an RVer.

"We could camp?" I say tentatively.

"Oh boy, yes!" says Dimitri, who I didn't think was listening. He's been tapping away on his laptop in front of the TV all night.

Spending a night in a tent with Mum and Dimitri? Um. That's pretty weird. But now that I've made the decision to go to the concert, I really want to go. And Dimitri is the only guy I know who has camping equipment.

Mum looks between me and Dimitri. I can see her weighing her options. If she says no, she'll have to drive five hours in one day in her dodgy little car. If she says yes, she might actually have some fun, even if it means spending the night in a tent.

"Yes, all right," says Mum, rolling her eyes. "I'll see if I can get a campsite. At least it won't cost me five hundred and fifty dollars."

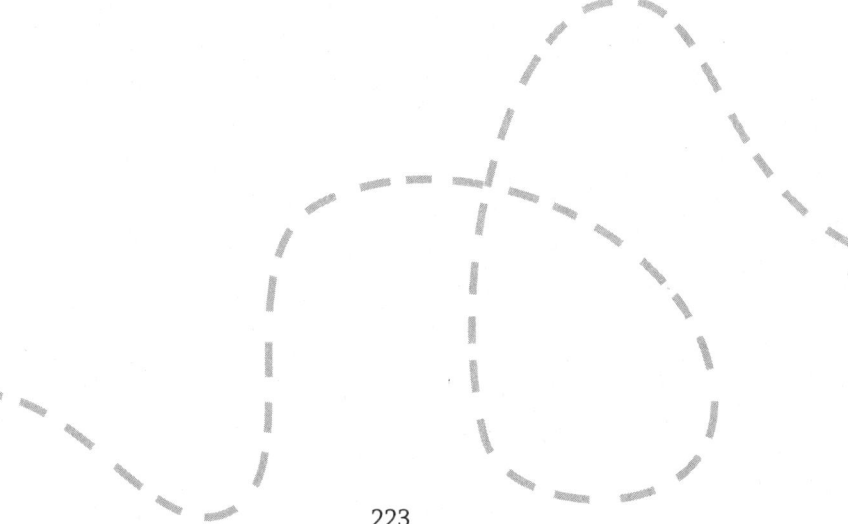

*the sixth move*

# THE TENT

# forty-two

**DIMITRI'S TENT, LIKE HIS HOUSE,** is a palace. Again, I have my own room. Wing, even. Just me, in my own section of the tent. Mum and Dimitri are sharing, which I'm finally almost getting used to. Sort of. Actually, in the last couple of weeks, I've been getting used to Dimitri and all his glossy ways.

Besides, Mum is happier than I've seen her in a really long time.

My Fender and Dad's guitar are perched next to me. I'm planning to play the Fender, because it's the better instrument. And presumably the competition has a proper amp and speakers. It will be pretty cool to crank up the volume and play my song to a whole crowd of people as if I'm a genuine rock star.

If I can ever get on the stage, that is.

I've brought Dad's guitar for comfort more than anything.

I've brought Dory, too, for comfort. That sounds weird. But I did end up emailing him to say sorry for storming off and could he please come along.

To: Dory E.
From: Queenie Jean
Subject: A humble apology
Hey, Dory,

I suck, and I'm sorry. I know you didn't mean to call me a loser. And I know you're just putting a boot in my bum, and that's exactly the kind of friend I want to have.

Please, pretty please come to the Summer Song Contest in Williams Head if your mum says it's okay. We're camping at Ripples Holiday Park in Williams Head if you are looking for a campsite.

Your mixing and mastering is unreal, by the way, and I am very lucky that we happened to bunk at the Elliots' and not some other random place.

Q.

To: Queenie Jean
From: Dory E.
Subject: A humble yes please
Hey, Queenie Jean,
    I am only coming on one condition. That I am allowed to wear the Queenie Jean band T-shirt and be your backup singer.
    D.

Dory will be there to back me up. Mum will be there, her twinkling eyes proud as mustard. Dimitri will be there 100 percent believing in me. So all that's left now is to show up. I listen to Billie. Then I listen to Queenie Jean. The ocean hums beside us.

A month or so ago, Queenie Jean Anderson might have known about the Summer Song Contest and fantasized about showing up. But she would have tucked herself into her little peach room, in her cozy bed, with her dad's guitar, and felt too comfortable to go anywhere. Because doing something cool like singing your own songs to a crowd requires being uncomfortable.

But the Queenie Jean who got herself all the way up to Williams Head now knows what it's like to be uncomfortable. She knows what it's like to share a single bed with your mum in a dead guy's unit. And what it's like to lead a choir of old people. She knows what it's like to fall for the chess guy from class and kiss his mouth even though she shouldn't. She knows what it's like to watch her stuff float around in a camper van. And to help a teacher study for her med school exams.

This Queenie Jean knows the discomfort of stepping aside so her favorite mum in the world can hold hands with the guy she likes.

Uncomfortable didn't kill Queenie.

Change didn't kill Queenie.

I know Queenie Jean will step out of the wings tomorrow night at five p.m. and sing "Summer Home"— her debut original—because change doesn't kill you: it makes you stronger.

## forty-three

**THE SUMMER SONG CONTEST IS SUPPOSED** to be held on the beach, on an outdoor stage. But the next morning, heavy clouds hang in the sky. The organizers have had to move the event to Williams Head Community Center.

Even though we've been downgraded to the community center, I'm relieved. I have been checking my email every minute, half expecting them to cancel the event because of COVID safety. Live music gigs are only just starting to happen again, and it still doesn't feel like they're for real.

But it's almost five p.m., and the song contest is going ahead.

There'll be no chickening out.

Mum squeezes my hand when we enter the dingy venue. She's carrying Dad's guitar for me. I have the Fender over my shoulder. I turn to catch Dory's eye. He grins and gives me a thumbs-up. Dimitri does, too. Frankie licks his chin.

There are loads of people filling the lobby. The adults are signing in with the COVID safety app. Everyone's sanitizing. It seems weird, seeing people rub germ protection into their hands, then stand shoulder to shoulder with twelve million strangers who could potentially give them COVID.

But this is COVID-normal.

And people have missed live music. We can share a few germs in the name of music.

Dory, Mum, Dimitri, and I sit in a row of plastic chairs about halfway back from the small stage. The stage is decorated with a banner: SUMMER SONG CONTEST with too many exclamation marks. Balloons hang off rafters.

"Queenie, Daisy texted to wish you luck," says Mum, passing over her phone for me to see.

Good luck, Queenie. Rock their socks off! Daisy

She signs off with a daisy emoji.

I half smile. It's the first I've heard from Daisy since we left Shoestring Creek.

I type back.

Thanks, Daisy. That's the plan. Hope GAMSAT study is going well. Queenie

I sign off with a crown and hand Mum back her phone.

I also have Audrey's scribbled note in my pocket.

*Go get 'em, Tiger. Love, Audrey and Walter*

I study the set list in the half dark. It's been photocopied on green paper, which is a bit amateurish, if you ask me. Amateurish or not, my throat feels dry seeing my name in print, directly next to my song's title: "Summer Home."

"Eleven's my lucky number," says Dory, grinning.

"Cool," I manage to say.

Three's my lucky number. And the name next to "three" fills me with heat.

Sparrow Hawkins.

Her song title, funnily enough, is also "Summer Home."

I jolt to my feet.

"Where are you going, Queenie?" asks Dory, looking surprised as I push past his long legs.

"Queenie!" calls Mum. "The show starts in five minutes, the lady said!"

"Bathroom!" I call back.

But I am not going to the bathroom.

I elbow through the crowd. I expect Sparrow to stand out. But she doesn't. I see a girl who I think might be her. But when she turns around, she completely isn't.

I am starting to wonder whether I manifested Sparrow's name on the set list as some sort of brain trick to get myself out of performing. I relook at the program.

Sparrow's name is still there.

My song's title is still next to it. Eight whole spots before Queenie Jean is going to get up and sing the same song at a contest that is meant to be all about originality. The judges will think Queenie Jean is a copier and a thief. They won't know that Sparrow is the real copier and thief.

Now that I know Sparrow's mirroring ways were intentional, I am seriously regretting sharing Frankie time with her. I should never have weakened and let her back into my life.

How could she have betrayed me like this? I just wish now that Dory hadn't uploaded my music to Spotify. Otherwise Sparrow wouldn't have had the opportunity to steal from me.

There's a static buzz as the speakers come to life. The announcer lady with bleached spiky hair leans into the mic.

"If everyone could take a seat, we are about to commence."

I do one last check of the bathrooms. But Sparrow is nowhere.

I reluctantly drag myself back to my chair. I am just going to have to endure watching my supposed friend sing my original song at the song contest.

The only solution now is to go out on a limb and sing a different song when it's my turn.

It's not as good as "Summer Home," but I'll sing "Victory." I like my newest song, "Mustard Seeds," better, but I know "Victory" is tighter. I've practiced it more. And I have the electronic backup for it on a flash drive in my pocket.

The first performer has an amazingly good voice. I have no idea where her huge voice is coming from, because she's teeny-tiny, like she just escaped out of a Polly Pocket. Her song, though, is average, if I am honest. It sounds a bit like it should be opening the *Teletubbies* rather than the Summer Song Contest.

The second performer is an older man with glasses and high-waisted jeans who reads his song lyrics from a little notepad.

The song's interesting. It's a bit country and western, about growing up in cotton country.

And then it's Sparrow's turn.

Dory's looking way too pleased about this. He's

tapping Sparrow's name in the program excitedly. "I can't believe Sparrow's here, too!" he says.

"I can," I say through gritted teeth.

"Oh, Sparrow Hawkins!" says Mum. "You were little friends in kindergarten! I always thought she had a great singing voice. What a coincidence she's here, too!"

"Not a coincidence," I say.

"Sparrow Hawkins?" says the announcer again. There's no Sparrow Hawkins anywhere to be seen. I nearly break my neck turning to try to see her in the crowd.

"Sparrow Hawkins? This is your final call." The lady's voice lingers. I am not the only one turning around. Seems like everyone is wondering where Sparrow is.

My heart slows when the next person is called. I wait for the satisfaction to set in. Sparrow has chickened out. Sparrow Hawkins has done a Queenie Anderson and has left the building.

But satisfaction doesn't come. Instead I find myself feeling . . . bad for Sparrow. What kind of person feels they need to steal their friend's song so blatantly?

My eyelids prickle. I am sorry for Sparrow. But I am also relieved. Not because she didn't get up to sing "Summer Home." But because we can still maybe be friends when all this is over.

## forty-four

**THE NEXT ACTS PASS IN A HAZE.** I can barely listen. Not for lack of interest or support. But because I am so darn nervous. And I think I am half expecting Sparrow to make a late entrance and demand her place on the stage.

Contestant number ten looks a lot like Dolly Parton. She's just about as old and wears cowgirl boots and everything. I have no idea what her song's about, though, because after I've kissed Frankie's head for good luck, I am squeezing past knees to try to get to the side of the stage. Mum follows me, carrying Dad's guitar, like a genuine groupie.

I stand in the wings gripping the Fender as if it's going to run out onstage and give me away.

What if I am terrible?

What if I stand there and no words come out? Like what happened to Audrey when she sang Frank Sinatra?

What if I can't get my legs to move and, like Sparrow, chicken out again?

This is my last opportunity. If I bail on this, I will know for sure that I can definitely never, ever perform music, and I will have to retreat to a cave and send my recordings to the world by email.

Dread doesn't feel like Antarctica. Or the Arctic. It feels like Neptune—the coldest planet in the solar system. All minus 214 degrees of awful.

"Queenie Jean?" says the announcer. Mum prods my back.

"Go, Queenie," she hisses. "Break a leg."

I stumble out onstage like the complete klutz that I am. I swear I am blinking like a deer, staring out into the audience.

I make out the fuzzy shape of Dory's hair in the dark.

I stare back at Mum. She's holding up Dad's guitar like a torch. "Dad would be proud of you," she whispers. "Do it for Dad, if not for yourself."

I turn and walk offstage.

"What are you doing?" hisses Mum. Her eyes are wobbly. "Don't do this to yourself, Queenie. You'll never forgive yourself. I promise you."

I hold in my smile. "I'm just switching guitars," I say. "I am going acoustic. For Dad."

I kiss Mum's cheek. She squeezes me.

"Ahem?" coughs the announcer, into the mic.

*Sorry,* I mouth as I walk back onstage carrying Dad's guitar, my stride confident and strong.

I'm doing this. I am actually doing this.

I nod to the sound guy, who's sitting at a desk to the side. He plugs in my flash drive, and the bass starts. I'm just about to play my first note when I hear a familiar voice call out to me from the wings.

"Queenie! I'm here!"

I spin around. Sparrow is jogging onstage.

*What are you doing?* I scream at her with my eyes.

I hear murmurs.

"Sorry I'm late. Traffic was horrible," she stage-whispers. She grabs the spare mic and props it in the stand next to me. I know my eyes are huge, staring at her in horror. Here I am onstage, about to sing. And here Sparrow is, too.

The tune's carrying on without me. I've missed the first verse. Sparrow, however, joins in with the second verse. In harmony.

I sing.

I finally sing. My voice breaks but settles, and I am singing my heart out, staring into the world, as if the audience isn't even there. All I can hear are Sparrow's beautiful harmonies, weaving into my tune, making "Summer Home" a million times better.

When we are done, Sparrow lifts my arm—a champion's salute. She points at me. The crowd cheers. My chest swells. My eyes sting. I glance at Mum, holding the Fender for dear life, mascara tracks the whole way down her face.

I just sang onstage. It didn't even kill me. But it definitely made me stronger.

## forty-five

**SPARROW AND I ARE SHARING A PLASTIC SEAT.** Dory's squeezing my knee so hard. But I don't feel it. Mum's squeezing my hand.

And then the Summer Song Contest is over. The lights buzz on. Parents and contestants stand and head to the bar for water and other beverages while we wait for the judges to make their decision.

"Sorry I was so late!" says Sparrow. "We hit traffic on the M1. I told Mum we needed to leave before three!"

I shake my head and show her the program.

"You were scheduled to play my song," I say. "Or did we coincidentally just have the same song title?"

Sparrow laughs. "Queenie. Honestly, you are hilarious sometimes. I came here to sing with you, you nincompoop. Didn't you hear me up there? I've been practicing since Dory sent me your songs on Spotify. I could tell you needed backup."

I shoot Dory a look. I can't tell if I am mad or ecstatic.

"I didn't need your help," I say. "I can sing fine."

"Of course you can! You're amazing. I just thought, well. I thought it wouldn't hurt. Give me that." Sparrow studies the program. "They must have got my voicemail all mixed up. I rang to ask if I could be your backup for 'Summer Home,' not sing my own version of it."

She hands me back the program.

I am a nincompoop.

I turn to face Sparrow, full on, so she can see every part of my face.

"Thank you, Sparrow. You were amazing. I did need you one hundred percent, and if we don't win, the judges are fools."

Sparrow grins, her mouth full of teeth, and I think I might just have my best friend back.

o o o

The cotton farmer takes the trophy. Dimitri raises the injustice every five minutes after we cram into the booths at the local burger joint.

I glance out at Frankie, who is outside looking in mournfully. Poor pup.

"I just don't understand it!" says Dimitri. "The lyrics made no sense. And the delivery was woeful. You and Sparrow stole the show, Queenie!"

"But I mucked up an entire verse," I say. "The judges can't reward that kind of behavior. That wouldn't be fair."

The real fact of it all is that I truly don't mind. Not a bit. I could have come in last for all I care. Because I have already won.

I sang onstage. My original song. People clapped and cheered. And now I am here, with a bunch of people who like me, and I like them, and a little pooch on the other side of the window.

I raise a glass.

"To the cotton farmer," I say.

*the seventh move*

# HERITAGE
# GARDENS

## forty-six

**MUM IS RIGHT. HERITAGE GARDENS** isn't a retirement village, even though it looks suspiciously like one. There's a family living in the unit next door. Two kids, a boy and a girl named Vic and Charlotte. Charlotte is one year older than me and goes to my school, and Vic is one year younger than me. Even though we only moved in yesterday, we've already gone swimming together, because it's the last day of summer break and it was a million degrees today. The kids, on the other hand, both seem pretty cool.

Mum and Dimitri are cuddling on the couch. Dimitri's feet are on an upturned box, which is for now our coffee table. There's a half-eaten container of butter chicken on the floor next to him. I'm leaning against Mum's knees, with Frankie stretched out like a furry sausage on my lap.

We're watching *RuPaul's Drag Race*.

"You feeling okay about starting at your new school tomorrow, Queenie?" asks Dimitri while we're waiting for the next episode to start. "The upper school is kind of a big deal."

"It is," I say. "But all my friends will be there."

All my friends. Dory. Sparrow. And now Charlotte, my neighbor.

It's true. I do feel fine about starting big school. I have my big-girl pants on, and my big-girl songs are out in the world, making a life for themselves. One of them—"Mustard Seeds"—already has 252 plays!

I've fallen in love with a boy. Gained a stepdad person. And moved seven times over the summer.

What's starting at a new school?

"I'm going to my room," I say, tucking Frankie under my arm. "Will leave you two lovebirds to it." Mum giggles and sheepishly nuzzles Dimitri's neck.

Back in my room, I open up my email. I grin. Dory's sent the latest master for "Queenie in Seven Moves," my newest track.

I press my headphones to my ears. The song rushes into me.

Sparrow's harmonies sound amazing. I can't believe I ever doubted her.

Here in my new home, I play the track again and close my eyes. Frankie sinks into me.

*Home cut from diamonds. Diamonds from sand.*
*You sink when you fall. And you'll rise where you stand.*
*You'll sing your heart out,*
*Sing to the sky.*
*New friends will be there to come see you try.*

*Home made on shoestrings. Vans full of flood.*
*You fall when it sinks. And leave there for good.*
*You'll laugh with eyes open,*
*Sing to the sky.*
*And new friends will be here to come see you try.*

*Home in a tent. Home with a pool.*
*Home comes in all shapes. Is nobody's fool.*
*You'll take yourself with you, wherever you go,*
*So take the right person*
*Who promised to grow.*

I smile. Hang my headphones on the computer. Give Frankie a scratch behind the ear.

*Queenie Jean Anderson can come with me wherever I go,* I think.

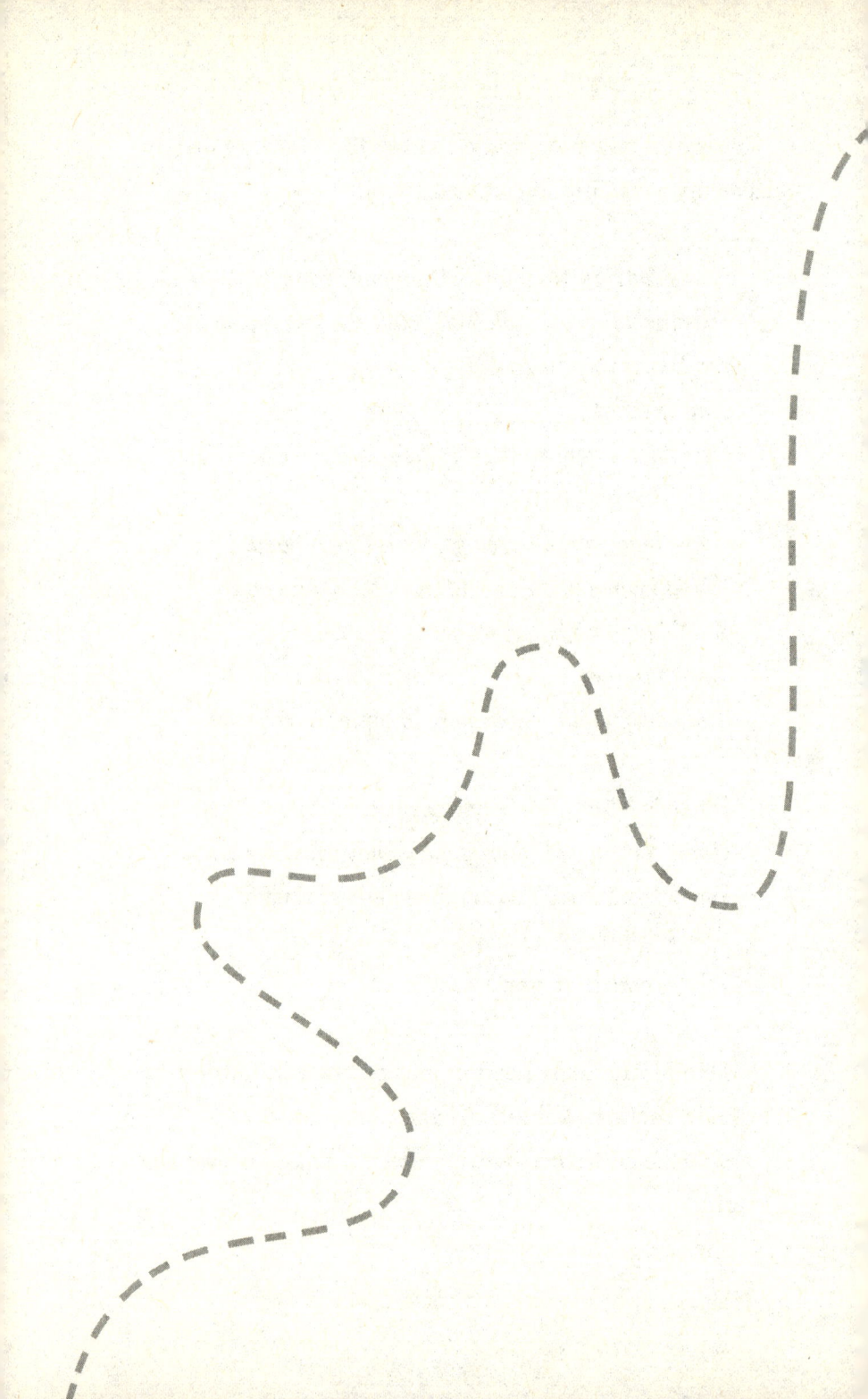

# acknowledgments

In 2019, my little family and I were living on a beautiful rural property in the Byron Bay hinterland in New South Wales, Australia. We were surrounded by neighbors whose kids were the same age as my kids. Pre-pandemic, the kids would meet in the nearby field and hang out in the trees to chat for hours. It was a happy time.

The pandemic set in and next thing we knew, our beloved property was for sale. We had tenants in our own home, so we started looking for a rental. It wasn't easy to find a place to rent as people were moving up from Sydney in droves, trying to escape spending lockdown in the city. We gave away our cat, Mary, to make it easier. But still, there were too many people to contend with.

Fortunately, friends put us up in their studio, shed, one-bedroom flat . . . We lived out of suitcases and in one summer moved seven times.

I'd occasionally drive past our old property, a knot of sadness in my chest for all the things we'd lost. But we'd also gained so much, too. A love of living lightly. Reading for hours on beanbag chairs. Stepping outside our comfort zones. Accepting people's generosity and becoming closer to our friends.

As I passed the old place one day, Queenie's story unfolded like a concertina. I rushed home, rang my writing friend Kiah Thomas, and told her the idea.

"Write it. Write it now," she said.

So I did. I cleared my calendar and wrote until I'd finished the first draft.

Thank you to the wonderful families who put us up that summer: the Altices, the McAllisters, and the Armytages. Your generosity will always be remembered, and those weeks together are treasured.

Thank you to Kiah for giving me the confidence to write Queenie's story and validating me the whole way through. For our long walks together and the many plot holes you helped me untangle and restitch. Thank you for helping me find my voice.

Thank you to the Uber Talented Writing Group: Tristan Bancks, Sarah Armstrong, Deborah Abela, and Lian Tanner, for your monthly endorsement and for essentially teaching me how to write a middle-grade novel. Your support means everything.

Thank you to my parents, Richard and Margaret, who, like Queenie's mum, have always given me space and encouragement to do the things I love—like writing.

Thank you to Linsay Knight from Walker Books, who read my book on a Sunday and signed it up that week. You changed my life in a matter of days, and I'll be eternally grateful. And to Clare Hallifax for the support you continue to give me now that Linsay has retired.

Thank you to Suzanne O'Sullivan for the most pleasant editing experience I could have wished for.

Thank you to Jo Hunt for the beautiful cover and to the whole team at Walker Books for your support.

Thank you to my aunt, Hendrika Johnson, who kindly read scenes set at Diamonds and checked for credibility using her vast experience working in the aged care sector.

Thank you to my friends who have supported my writing career since it began as a seed and who continue to buy my books for your children.

Thank you to my wonderful children's book community: the Sunshine House and beyond. Thank you for your endless warmth and support.

Special thanks to my daughters, Elka and Eve, who not only helped inform Queenie's character and taste in music but who also endlessly inspire and bring me happiness. And to Gregor, my partner, who's fanned my creative flames from the beginning, supported me in every way he knows how, and has now brought Queenie's songs to life. For real. To Brett Canning, too, for your music production. Thank you also to the wonderful booksellers, librarians, teachers, and parents who are passionate about putting quality books into kids' hands.

Thank you most especially to you—the reader. Without you, this book would not exist.

# listen to Queenie Jean

Scan the QR code to listen to "Home"
and "One Long Summer's Day"
by Queenie Jean.